Herkimer's Nose

a Kingston Story

by Richard Schwindt

This book is a work of fiction. The characters, incidents and dialogue are drawn from the author's imagination and are not to be construed as real. Any resemblance to actual events or persons, living or dead, is coincidental.

That being said…

Nicholas Herkimer (also spelled Herchmer) was a real person. His temperment and character are fictionalized.

Finkle's tavern was built in 1793; one of the first brewpubs in Upper Canada. Unlike modern brewpubs, it doubled as a courthouse, being the site of one of the first trials in Eastern Ontario, where a transient, falsely accused of stealing a watch, was convicted and hanged on the spot.

Moses Rogers was a real person, but he escaped from jail and his eventual whereabouts remain a mystery. Many believe he fled to the U.S.

I have no idea if William Lemoine drank, or the circumstances of his drowning while sledding.

I live in Kingston and often visit Queens University. They mostly seem like real places. Same with Scarborough.

I haven't a clue about the ichthyology program - or if they even have one at Queens University. That said, numerous scientists work to control the depredations of invasive species in the Great Lakes.

This book is intended as entertainment. Many of my books have serious intent, and redeeming social value. This is not one of them.

Be prepared for amusing banter, cartoonish violence, puerile sexual innuendo and swearing.

Table of Contents

October 1809
Bath, Ontario

…after Captain Herkimer's death in 1795, his third son Nicholas, a farmer, inherited the property and held it till his death in 1809 when he was murdered in Bath by two blacksmiths.

Cataraqui Region Conservation Authority website
History of Lemoine Point

Nicholas died in 1809 and was probably buried on his own property.
Alvin Armstrong

Buckskin to Broadloom
Nobody owns life, but anyone who can pick up a frying pan owns death.
William S Burroughs

Following farm transactions in Adolphustown, he had been driving the pony cart towards home. When the sky darkened he stopped for food, drink and sleep at Finkle's tavern.

He was in funds from business and benevolent enough to buy a round for the house. A landowner known for generosity, he'd displayed a wad of currency.

Later, as the beer, noise and smoke began to pall, he stepped out of doors for a moment to stand in solitude. A cold night; the air was still and crisp. Horses snorted and snuffled in the stable.

"Buy me another drink you stingy bastard." A short, stout man, with lank blonde hair appeared from the gloom before him with his hand out.

"If I must," the man said, laughing. He looked closer. "You need to work harder at that Smithy, Moses Rogers. But if I have to… here now, there's no call for that!"

Moses Rogers had pulled a dagger and pointed it at him. He could see the blacksmith's steaming breath by the light of the tavern. "Just give us your money, and we'll be on our way."

"We?"

An axe handle fell on his head even as Rogers stepped forward and thrust the knife into his belly. After a brief shining moment of pain, all went dark.

June, 1999
Somewhere over Southeastern Ontario

"The guide says there is an art to flying," said Ford, "or rather a knack. The knack lies in learning to throw yourself at the ground and miss."
Douglas Adams

"And to think they call me Speedy Gonzales."

Major Joe "Speedy" Gonzales looked up from the controls over to Second Lieutenant Veronica Mills and caught her chuckling.

"That's not funny, Second Lieutenant." The grin vanished from her face but he was only getting started:

"Fifty F-16 missions in the two Gulf wars and the Balkans; 5 Mig kills, and I'm driving a goddam *Cessna Caravan* over Southern Ontario."

Mills was green, and intimidated by the decorated officer beside her but she tried to push back and stroke his ego at the same time.

"Sir, this may be a Cessna but we are also flying a covert plasma cannon cross country. If we can't get it in unnoticed through a friendly jurisdiction, how are we going to get it through enemy territory?"

She stopped and looked at the pilot. He wasn't mollified.

As if by instinct they both turned back to the Weapon's Operator - Technical Sergeant Steven Weymann - and his console, which had emerged from behind a seat after take-off from Peterborough, Ontario forty minutes earlier.

No one wore a uniform. They had flown from upstate New York to Peterborough in the morning, posing as a group of friends out to enjoy a pleasure flight, and a visit to relations in Canada.

After an uneventful journey the plane landed at the local airport, they stepped through customs and took a cab out to lunch with operatives. The military had plotted this foray in various forms at different times, but today was the first trip with the actual weapon.

They had taken a calculated risk and left the plane, though two armed undercover combat controllers never lost sight of it.

Still this was Canada and not a dangerous mission. In a moment they would be over Kingston where Gonzales would land, refuel, take off again, and then set a vector across Lake Ontario towards home.

Mills felt obliged to continue: "Sir, this weapon can irradiate ten thousand people with one pulse. Who else would Operations assign to move it around?" She was rewarded with a small upturning of Gonzales's mouth.

"Sir!" A nervous voice interrupted Mills and Gonzales.

"What do you want, Weymann?" said the cranky pilot, "You're baggage on this trip, remember?"

"Sir, the weapon is powering up."

"Ha, don't fuck with me, Weymann, I'm not that bored."

"No…sir, the weapon is powering up; I estimate it will go off in three minutes."

"Jesus and Mary, Weymann, un-power the goddam thing; we're almost over a fucking Canadian city."

"I'm trying, I can't get it to respond. I must have touched the wrong button."

"Hit it!"

A sound resonated from the back as the desperate airman thumped the computer.

"Nothing sir, still powering up. Ninety seconds to firing sequence. I can't control it."

Mills eyes widened in horror.

She jerked sharply to starboard.

Gonzales banked the Cessna hard, while pushing the throttle to full.

God, Mills thought, he's going to run us straight into the lake! Mills didn't know what a Cessna Caravan could do when pushed to the max.

She was about to find out.

The small craft hurtled towards the surface. She had no idea this little plane could go so fast or generate so many G's. But then, gravity was helping.

They were fifty metres over empty water when the weapon fired.

Somehow Gonzales bounced off the recoil and achieved the lift he needed.

Minutes later the Cessna reached one thousand feet altitude over the lake, cruising towards home.

Ignoring the chatter from Air Traffic control in Kingston, trying to catch her breath, Mills turned back: "Weymann, take that fucking thing off line now! If we set Syracuse on fire, I'll have your fucking head!"

Now she took a breath.

Weymann was stammering to himself, white as a ghost.

Gonzales grinned madly, like he'd just won the lottery. She gave him a nudge. He turned.

"Sir, I think *that's* why they assigned this flight to you."

2017

Lemoine Point

Kingston, Ontario

"Herr Schiller? Are there really such things as ghosts?"
The old man did not even show surprise at the question.
He heaved a sigh. "Yes Pia, there are.
But never the ones you expect."
Helen Grant

"Call me Nick if you like! You'll find me hanging about most days, and years. Pull up a bench and chat for a spell. The things I could tell you!"

Who am I kidding? I have lots of time to listen but I hardly ever chat. Once every forty years or so someone shows up who can talk to me. The last one was old Maracle; Indian guy, funny as hell and great company.

We shared a lot of laughs until they showed up one day and hauled him away for wandering the park and talking to himself. Nervous onlooker I guess; thought he was batshit.

He came back once to tell me he'd been in the Provincial mental asylum down the lake in Kingston proper. Said he couldn't come back to visit me again or they would lock him up longer; sad day that; never saw him again.

I run into Bill Lemoine but he's usually looking out on the lake, pointing a spectral finger, pissing and moaning about his lost sled. I was watching while he was still alive - drank like a fish; no wonder he managed to drown during the winter of '72.

They named the park - *Lemoine Point* - after him; not me. Still resent that, but I guess the old name - *Herkimer's nose*

- was too strange for the populace. Shame really; people; lovers, depressives, reprobates, families, fools, drunks and conspirators wander the trails and woods with no sense of the real history.

And I listen; I always listen.

I have someone to talk to now - Courtney. She's really smart and a looker too! But I may have scared her away. I hope she comes back.

Saturday, July 1, 2017
Ellerbeck Street
Kingston, Ontario

My favorite moments?
Where it's all going swimmingly,
the suns out and I've got a fire going,
and a nice snake on the barbeque
Bear Grylls

When Doctor Messi accepted me into his Ichthyology lab to complete my post-doctoral research, it was the best day of my life. Contributing to the management of *Petromyzon marinus* is important work; we can never fall behind invasive species if we want to maintain the integrity of the Great Lakes.

Queens doesn't have the largest Ichthyology program in the country but it does have Fredriche Messi and that is enough.

Fredriche is brilliant and sweet but he's also stoned six days out of seven and obsessed with all things *fish*. After my first week in the lab he invited me to his house for a fish fry with his wife and a few friends.

He inhabits one of the multi-story houses on the west side of the campus, set among old maples, matted grass and unctuous professionals who drive Subarus and Beemers.

Old Kingston comes replete with the universities, military, limestone buildings, an affluent and educated populace, and a dark history; including penitentiaries, pestilence, murder, hangings, and ghostly memories.

"What's on the menu?" I asked, after accepting a glass of wine on the deck.

"*Petromyzon marinus,*" he said. "It's delicious if cooked properly. You will love it!" He was all excited, dressed in cut-offs; a reefer bobbing between his teeth.

"We're eating lamprey eel? Where did you get it?"

"Out of lab; I don't have time for fishing."

I was new and didn't want to say anything but our research focused on creative ways of poisoning the damn things; I didn't want to *eat* anything out of his lab.

He turned to a fortyish woman who resembled a constipated librarian and continued a conversation on viscera.

Fredriches' wife, Brittany waved at me from behind the French doors. A petite and pretty woman, dressed in hippie clothes, she had adorned herself with turquoise and Indian red bangles.

"Excuse me," I said to no one in particular, "I can help with the salad."

Inside, she took my arm and pulled me to the countertop. A sly grin formed on her face. She glanced out the kitchen window at the party on the deck.

"He means well," she said, starting with an apology, "but this comes up every barbeque season."

Then in a more conspiratorial tone: "He'll be fixated on the barbeque. I keep the salad in here. I tell him it stays fresher inside."

She pointed to a covered bowl and said: "breaded squid." I must have looked confused.

"When he ladles the slime-eel onto your plate, tell him you are going for salad. Come in here, scrape the plate under the sink and scoop the squid onto a new plate. Take your salad and return to the deck."

She waited for a moment, peeked outside again, and finished:

"Lamprey tastes like it looks. He's pretty stoned this time of day and drinking Merlot; he'll never know the difference."

She paused as if to ensure she had told me everything then returned to the last item. "More wine?"

As she filled my glass, I looked out the window. Fredriche is tall, on the thin side, and peers out at the world through thick round glasses. He moves about awkwardly and my thought was; watch him at the barbeque long enough and you would see him burn something, likely himself.

I wondered what the attraction was between him and Brittany.

"He's great in the sack," she said, as if reading my mind. I wanted to say: "Too much information," but laughed instead. "And he knows a lot about fish."

I looked over at her serious face. I knew nothing about them; no kids running around. Surely she wasn't be interested in fish?

"Gotcha," she said with a quick grin. "I cut hair for a living. Making fun of academic types helps me cope."

There was mischief but no malice in her tone so I laughed again.

Then on impulse I gave her a hug and said thanks.

"You're cool," I told her.

"And you're different," she said. I looked into those deep blue eyes and I understood. I can always tell.

"Do people know?"

She shook her head; so I drew a finger across my lips. After another quick hug I returned to the deck.

Following the stealth squid, more wine appeared and our jolly evening became looser and funnier as we drank into the crepuscular dusk.

By dark everyone was drunk. Surrounded by walls of lilac and the soft hum of crickets - talking loud; our laughter filled the night.

As the birds stilled, the first bats flitted from among the trees.

"Where are you from?" the fish guts lady asked me out of nowhere. I turned to her and smiled. She spoke with an edge, but I'd drank too much to catch it.

"Scarborough," I said, oblivious to the change in expression on her face.

"I can't imagine how you put up with the crime," she said in a condescending tone, "I hear there are guns and a great deal of violence."

"Oh, that's not what Scarborough is about." I carried on, smiling, deaf to nuance. "The parks and the waterfront are so beautiful, lots of great people … and…"

"You can't deny that it is a troubled community, can you?"

Now I felt stupid.

I wanted to take her on but a group had gathered and the lady - I didn't even know her damn name yet - dropped me and addressed the crowd:

"Hello everyone, my name is Doctor Diane Naylor." I looked around; who the hell was she with this pompous intro; we all had doctorates, just fucking Diane would do.

I didn't like her and working on a good alcoholic shine; I needed to bite my tongue. I remembered Brittany who wasn't an egghead like the rest of us; and saved me from the greased Lamprey supper.

She stood by the doorway biting her lower lip. A glance told me that if I didn't like *Doctor* Diane, Brittany loathed her. We made eye contact and the corners of her mouth turn upwards as she silently intoned: "Skank".

Their house is on the west side of the Queens campus, with tall dark brick buildings on leafy avenues. People grow herb gardens and grill vegetables drizzled in extra virgin olive oil on well-scrubbed expensive barbeques.

"As you are aware," Doctor Diane continued, "every year we hold this barbeque and ask everyone to share something special about themselves - something unique."

She started with herself. "I want to share that I am reading a fascinating paper on recovery of proteinases and protein hydrolysates from fish viscera."

Oh Fuck, confessions of a fish geek. Not sure I could handle her uniqueness.

That out of the way, she gestured towards Brittany.

"I can tell right away who went grey in their twenties," Brittany said, with the air of someone who had resigned herself to this nonsense. But she looked straight at Doctor Diane.

"Fredriche?" Diane said, hastily turning towards our host.

"I secretly smoke marijuana," he said, revealing the lamest secret in Kingston. Everyone laughed.

"And our newest guest - post doctoral Fellow, Courtney Snow... from Scarborough."

Everyone looked at me.

I acted on impulse, driven by the Merlot, and only one person guessed what was coming.

Brittany shook her head, mouthing - "*DON'T*", but it was too late. The words had already exited my mouth.

"I am a medium," I said. And to be clear to the over-educated audience: "I see dead people."

Not to pun, but that stopped everyone dead. People stared; *is the new chick making a joke? She looks serious enough.* It became awkward, then Diane spoke:

"That's very amusing Courtney, well, let's carry on - Doctor Barret?"

Later, alone with Brittany, she was cross. We were in the kitchen; I was the only one to think of helping with the dishes.

She lit candles to make it cozy; the guests had departed and Fredriche passed out on the couch. She appreciated my company but couldn't help chewing me out.

"What were you thinking? You seem like a nice person, I hope we become friends but you are lucky they didn't believe you." She reached for a glass of Merlot; the night was her time.

"What kind of psychic are you?" I asked.

"I have the gift of discernment - I know stuff. I don't know how I know stuff but I do."

Then she added: "I don't see dead people or anything." She shuddered; the thought did not appeal.

"It's not so bad. I can usually tune them out and most of them are more lost than anything else. You do meet the occasional asshole."

Two months earlier
Lemoine Point Conservation area
West Kingston

Bordered by Lake Ontario and Collin's Bay, Lemoine Point is 136 hectares of forest, field and marsh, with a spectacular waterfront. Many opportunities for recreation and nature appreciation are available in all seasons.

Website of Cataraqui Region Conservation Authority

The muses are ghosts and sometimes they come uninvited.
Stephen King

If you drive through the north entrance, early on a weekday morning, the light pierces to your left through the canopy of maple and oak. You have the rolling land to yourself before the dog walkers and seniors arrive.

Nature wakes early; birds twitter and plump squirrels run about, hoarding seeds left by visiting children.

I love the solitude and the regeneration that comes from woodland rambles; and just being away from the University. But this Tuesday morning, warm for the season, was destined to take a strange turn.

I wore a loose tee-shirt with jeans; which left me cool and invigorated.

A man approached, hurrying, from the opposite direction.

He wore tight knee breeches, a linen shirt, knitted wool stockings, and heavy shoes. And a tall top hat made of felt.

His face sported - I guess the word is side whiskers - huge and bushy - highlighting bright cobalt blue eyes.

Clueless, I assumed he was an actor and a historical activity must be underway further along the path. I contemplated saying hello but valued my alone time enough to ignore him.

He spoke instead:

"Whoa, nice boobies baby doll!"

I wouldn't ignore that, and my response escaped before I had a chance to think: "Put a lid on it, asshole."

He stopped so abruptly it was as if he had hit a wall. I felt scared and aware that I was alone on an empty path.

But his face registered neither anger nor lust; in fact, he looked more shocked than anything else.

Then the penny dropped.

"Oh…" I said. His gaze cantilevered from my breasts to my eyes. For a moment his eyes filled with unbearable sadness. Then the smirk returned.

"You can see me?" he said.

"And hear you. Your manners die with you?"

"You're not supposed to hear me."

"You call that an excuse? You don't talk to women that way, period." He looked mortified; so mortified that I felt sorry for him. He *was* dead.

And to my surprise, he apologised:

"I am very sorry for my rudeness… what did you say your name was?"

"Courtney."

"Courtney, forgive my foul mouth and rough-hewn ways."

I felt better.

"And your name?"

"Nicholas - Nick Herkimer. Used to own this place." He gestured broadly at the park surrounding us.

"I thought it was a guy named Lemoine?" He rolled his eyes and dramatically clapped a hand to his forehead.

"That soak came *after* me and let me tell you - he was *never* sober enough to even *know* he owned the land. If you don't believe me, go ask him yourself; he's still staring out at the lake."

I'd hit a nerve, but one ghost was enough.

"Listen Nick, we got off to a bad start but I accept your apology. I have to go; see you around."

"When?" I turned. I wanted to tell him to piss off but couldn't. He continued: "I do a lot of listening but I hardly ever get to talk."

"I wish my last boyfriend was more like you."

"If you want to come by and chat, I'll be here - with my manners. I'm always around and … it would be nice; it's been about fifty years since my last two way conversation.

"I could tell you all kinds of things. I've been listening to everyone for two hundred years. If someone's had a confidential chat in the woods, I've been right there."

Then he surprised me. "I'm guessing you are a scholar, up at the University.

"I'm in Ichthyology; you don't know what that is. You probably think women shouldn't work."

He put a finger to his temple, eyes turning upwards, as if searching from a deep memory bank.

"Why, I believe it is the study of the physiology, history and economic ramifications of fishes…

"And no woman worked harder than my Charlotte Purdy; you think it was easy to bear ten children and manage a farm?"

"It must have been a hard life…" Now he was making me feel ridiculous.

"Oh, not so bad; every Saturday night she'd come to bed just wearing her bonnet and carrying a ruler - cosplay you call it now - I'd pretend to be surprised that the school mistress was…"

"Gaak, I have to go." I turned to make a dignified exit and found myself face to face with an elderly couple.

"Are you all right, Miss?" the man said. He and his wife looked concerned. "We can drive you somewhere if you want."

They only saw me. My back was to Nick; I couldn't see him, but he was laughing so hard that he snorted. It sounded so funny I laughed too.

This wasn't helping my case with the kindly old folks so I deemed it a good time to make for my car.

Driving back downtown, I tried to have stern thoughts about the bad man but kept giggling to myself.

1300 hours
Saturday, July 8th
Water treatment plant
Kingston

You are disoriented. Blackness swims towards you like a school of eels who have just seen something eels like a lot.
Douglas Adams

On torpid afternoons, the Jeunesse Dorée liked hang at the dock outside the water treatment plant, on Lake Ontario, across from the Queens campus. Some hung out in skimpy swimwear, some swam and a few kite surfed.

Others ate, drank, smoked weed and practised mating rituals. Life under the lurid sun was good.

Drew Whitman tossed long blond locks away from his forehead as he gazed out at the lake. Wolfe Island sat across the water, and Sunfish sailboats skittered over the light waves. His tanned body gleamed.

Weed, sashimi - and Kayla Cooper, waiting for him in residence. Was this even real? A single baleful cloud hung on the horizon; Drew felt sad for it. Time for one more dip, then back to Kayla.

Without further reflection Drew dove off the cement dock and into the cold water, chilling his body as he paddled under the surface.

Cory Smythe, facing a similar hedonistic near term, gazed at the water, with occasional glances to his girlfriend, Kelly-Anne who, clad in a chartreuse bikini, stared out at the day. It was too beautiful.

"Did you see that?" she said. He followed her pointing hand. Nothing. Then something.

Something like a pipeline; no, a greyish snake but whoa, it was fucking immense.

"Oh my God," Kelly-Anne said. Cory was struck dumb. A head appeared; something from a nightmare; a hideous gaping orifice filled with hundreds of encircling teeth.

The size of a small car, the head appeared, turned about, and dove beneath the waves. When it came up again, the mouth puckered around the thrashing body of Drew Whitman.

Kelly-Anne retched and Cory fell to his knees. Others were looking now; people screamed, dialed cell phones and fell over faint.

Some of the students would be traumatized for years; a few quit university; none of them swam in a lake again that summer. And one, Drew Whitman, never drew another breath.

1330 hours
Offshore, Kingston Harbour

Take charge of your life!
The tides do not command the ship. The sailor does.
Ogwo David Emenike

The Canadian Coast Guard Cape Class motor lifeboat *LaSalle* was anchored minutes away. Captain Philip Vukcic stood on the desk as the vessel approached the Water Treatment Plant.

He shouted down to the Engineer, Martha Spatafora: "Anything?"

Spatafora had eyes on sonar and reported: "Nothing; not a damn thing."

Vukcic pointed the binoculars towards the shore. He then put his glasses down and shouted at his Engineer again: "It's a mess on the beach."

Paramedics shooed kids away, people filmed with cell phones; sirens blared, lights flashed and a bloody bundle lay at the center. Even a hundred metres offshore it was easy to see red lapping onto the sand.

Stepping below, Vukcic continued: "Lets run a grid over the harbour. I have no idea what we are looking for but if it's here we need to find it."

"We're looking for a lake monster, sir," said the engineer. "That's what the kids said."

Vukcic was a practical man; he took his duty seriously. Despite his stern manner and swarthy appearance he was liked by the crew.

Martha Spatafora appreciated that he never gave her shit about her being a woman and an engineer.

One of the ensigns had taken a grab at her ass while they were surveying Howe Island. Vukcic had picked him up, thrown him over the side, watched him swim to shore, and left him to find his own way back.

She could live with his bluntness.

"There's no lake monster, Spatafora. But something killed that kid." He turned and shouted to one of the deckhands: "Baker, you got your phone?"

"Aye sir."

"Put it to good use for once; get Kingston Utilities on the blower and find out if they have loose power lines or anything else that could explain this." Baker's voice drifted down:

"Sir, it might be from the island." Wolfe Island lay across the harbour, defaced by turbines generating electricity from the lake winds.

"Okay, call Ontario Power Generation as well."

Vukcic returned to the deck and again trained his binoculars on the shoreline. The body stowed; an ambulance pulled away from the other emergency vehicles. He glanced at the new signage: the beach was closed.

0200 hours
Sunday, July 9th
Ichthyology Lab, Queens University

That's because it's from the night and the night keeps secrets.
Maggie Stiefvater

"It's not a fucking lamprey."

If Fredriche wouldn't say something I would.

"The largest lampreys in the water aren't two metres long, and while there are anecdotal stories of attacks on humans, they prefer their food cold blooded."

The men in the lab stared. I took a drink from my coffee, flicked on another light, and pointed at the tanks. One of the men jumped when he spotted the eel eliding through the dark water.

I smiled.

His colleague shot him a glance.

"That's considered a large lamprey." I said.

Fredriche looked terrified; his goggled eyes glinted in the lamplight. His voice emerged as a whisper.

"Doctor Snow is right. There's no such thing as a thirty metre lamprey, let alone one that can eat most of an undergraduate in seconds."

Was that regret I heard in his voice?

Fredriche, a pure researcher, disliked undergrads. In a perfect world there would indeed be such a fish to cull the lower order of students.

Brittany called after midnight; upset, crying into the phone. I had been in Scarborough visiting my parent's grave. I had only been asleep for an hour.

"Courtney, I'm so glad you answered; they took Fredriche away!"

Groggy and confused, I looked at my bedside clock and asked the obvious question:

"Who took him away?"

"A bunch of serious looking men and some cops. It has something to do with the kid killed today."

"What kid?"

"A Queens student was killed, in the water across from the campus."

"What's that go to do with Fredriche?"

"I don't know but they took him to the slime fish lab. He's really stoned; can you help him? They wouldn't let me; maybe you can go as a colleague."

So I dressed, went down to the car, swung by Tim Horton's for a large double-double, and then proceeded straight to the lab.

I couldn't imagine a creepier place on a murky night. Turn left at the limestone alley, tiptoe under the ancient ash tree, climb the stone stairs…

To make matters worse, Fredriche had taken them to the wet room. They all stood by the light of a single lamp. I could hear the swishing whispers of lampreys making serpiginous turns in their tanks.

Introductions were vague; two of the men were police detectives; two were from an obscure government department.

I couldn't believe what they had to say.

A thirty metre lamprey eel had attacked and mostly consumed a young man in front of a few dozen other young people this afternoon. What could we tell them about lampreys attacking humans?

That's when I lost my shit.

The guy who glanced at his jumpy colleague stepped forward and took this moment to properly introduce himself.

"I'm Doctor Truman. I am not an ichthyologist but do have a PhD in bioengineering. This is Kingston Detective Lang, and OPP Detective Tran. And this is Mr. Smith."

The last man stepped into the light. The one who had jumped. Shorter than the others, he had a stocky frame and short blonde hair.

"What do you do?" I asked.

"If I told you I'd have to kill you." Take one cliché and joke, add a spooky context and a straight face.

I looked closer. I think he was serious. The detectives looked away.

"Doctor Snow, can you boot up a computer?"

Five minutes later we were looking at a YouTube video shot by a student. Featuring terrified undergrads running and screaming; at first I thought they'd forgotten the lake monster, or even the water.

Then it appeared.

I am not the kind of scientist that rhapsodizes about the mysterious fractals and beautiful functionality of nature.

Few things in creation are as fucking ugly as the puss of a lamprey eel, especially when it's trying to suck the juice out of a student.

There was no mistaking the species though; this was *Petromyzon marinus,* writ large.

I felt afraid for the first time.

But no one was looking at me. All eyes were trained on the most distinguished ichthyologist in Eastern Canada.

Fredriche didn't hesitate to share his professional opinion: "*Whoa man, that's a big fish.*"

Embarrassed silence ensued, which I broke, addressing the men in the room:

"Is there a plan?"

Truman, who was studying the lampreys in the tank answered me:

"We've got the makings of an emergency task force in place. We are meeting tomorrow, ten am at the university conference center. All of us plus a few others, and the Navy. Can you both be there?

"Yes, Doctor Messi and I will be there. I think he may be a little shocked right now. I'm taking him home and we'll see you tomorrow."

0400 hours
Ellerbeck Street

Brittany was waiting at the door. She looked elfin and vulnerable.

"Is he okay?"

"I think he's a little stunned but I have something important to do and I need you with me."

"Right now? What about…"

"Just toss him on the couch. We have to be up early, and he needs to sleep off the weed."

Kingston Water Treatment Plant

The darker the night, the brighter the stars
The deeper the grief, the closer is God
Fyodor Dostoyevsky

The plant was only a short walk from Ellerbeck. Brittany wanted to know what we were doing.

The night remained calm and warm, but as we approached I saw small fires, candlelight; students were holding vigils. Some cried, a few talked with friends. I could smell weed in the air.

A half-moon hung in the distance, lighting the scattered clouds.

"I don't like the energy here," Brittany said. "These kids are confused and scared. The water feels polluted."

"I imagine it does." We reached the dock; I was searching for someone who appeared alone and confused. "I need you here so I don't look like I'm talking to myself."

"I don't under... oh, REALLY! That is so creepy." Her head started turning side to side. She didn't see him... but I did.

The ghost of Drew Whitman stood at the edge of the dock, looking out across the water. He was a handsome dude, but looked lost.

"Stand beside me and nod while I talk," I said to Brittany. "I won't look so weird that way." She nodded, still glancing around the dock.

"Hey Drew," I said, "How's it going?" I was pretty sure he wouldn't know he was dead.

"Oh hey, nice of you to say hello; everyone else is so snobby. Kayla's in a tent crying. She ignores me and won't even tell what I've done to piss her off."

"It's a lovely night," I said. "What's happening?"

"I think someone died. I don't know who; no one is talking to me."

I felt unbearably sad listening to this boy; he seemed too young to understand real pain.

"What's the last thing you remember?"

"Something while I was swimming; looked like a giant snake but all slimy. It was gross, man." He made a face.

"I want to ask an important question, Drew." He nodded but continued to gaze outwards. "Which direction did the snake come from; the side, or from straight out?"

Drew squinted then his eyes focused on something ahead. He saw something.

"Hey check out the light; it's so beautiful."

Oh crap, I didn't have much time.

"And there's my grandmother…"

"Drew, ignore the light…"

"I need to go now; nice talking to you… it's like a tunnel."

"Which direction?" But he'd gone.

"Dammit, dammit, dammit. He saw the bloody light and disappeared."

"He's gone to eternal rest, Courtney." Brittany, who wanted to sound a practical note; only heard one side of the conversation.

"He didn't tell you anything, did he?"

"No, I want to understand how this fish behaves; whether it's like other lampreys. The light could have waited."

"We need to go to bed."

1000 hours
Queens Conference Center

*Each meeting occurs at the precise moment
for which it is meant.
Usually when it will have the greatest
impact on our lives.
Nadia Scrieva*

Two surprises waited for us at the conference center; one good; one not so much.

The good surprise was Lieutenant-commander Marie Lesage from the Royal Canadian Navy. She seemed competent and bright. I was glad the Navy was worried enough to send a senior officer.

The not so good surprise took the form of the task force science director, one Doctor Diane Naylor.

"You will be under my supervision," she announced to Fredriche and me in front of the group. "We will need to stay on task."

Why the fuck was she in charge? I looked across the table. She had that Mussolini-like habit of thrusting out her chin when she talked.

Outside of a bad first impression, I knew nothing about her. I found it hard to believe she was a competent scientist, claims of dorkish reading habits to the contrary.

I glanced next at Fredriche. He still looked intimidated, glancing at the other participants, but displayed no signs of being high. Would he have something intelligent to say?

Truman took charge. Outside of shadowy lab he presented as confident and well put together. He wore an unwrinkled charcoal coloured suit. No one would have guessed he'd been up all night.

I thought he might be indigenous. His skin was an olive colour; he looked out at the world through sharp black eyes. His long hair belonged on a model, not a civil servant.

This thought created a self-conscious pang; God, my hair! When I woke up this morning, after two hours sleep, it had the texture of spaghetti deep fried in soy oil.

But I had to remember why I was sitting on a comfy chair sipping decent coffee. I had to remember the poor boy I'd seen last night.

"Thank you for coming today; special thanks to Lieutenant-commander Lesage who flew in early from Halifax. I don't have to tell you we are facing a unique crisis. Rumours are already circulating coast to coast.

"I'll move straight to the point. A twenty year old Queens student was attacked, killed and partially ingested yesterday afternoon by what appeared to be a giant lamprey eel.

"Doctors Messi and Snow tell me there is no precedent for this; the creature in question is way beyond any extant species of eel or similar fish."

"I can confirm that," Diane said.

By pressing my palms hard against the surface of the table I controlled my tongue. What were they paying her? But she wasn't done:

"We want to capture this animal and study it. Try to understand what makes it tick."

It was probably the visceral dislike I felt towards her, but I had to speak.

"What if they kill someone else? Maybe we should just shoot it and study the pieces. I don't think this thing belongs in nature. Even ordinary lampreys in Lake Ontario are a parasitic invasive species.

"Two levels of government designated our lab funding explicitly to take the little fuckers out. They almost destroyed the lake trout fishery in the 1940s and 50s."

"As the junior scientist here perhaps you should sit back and let us hear from others."

Thanks Diane. Bitch.

I shut up - not easily, or without anger - but I was mollified watching the Navy officer nodding out of the corner of my eye. She'd sworn to protect Canadians from outside threats, and if it took the form of a lake monster so be it.

Truman picked up on something I had said.

"Doctor Snow, did you say "they"? Are you suggesting there are more eels?"

Everyone looked at me again.

"We may have the sea lamprey under semi-control right now but a female can lay up to a hundred thousand eggs.

"There's emerging evidence they've developed tolerance to TFM - that's 3-trifluoromethyl-4-nitrophenol, the most common, lampricide. If it even works on a lamprey this big."

"I'm sure that people aren't interested in the scientific minutiae right now," said Diane.

"I'm interested," said Truman.

"Me too," said Lieutenant-commander Lesage. So I continued:

"The sea lamprey has survived four extinction events in world history – over 360 million years. It is robust, strong, and perfectly adapted for latching on to other sea creatures and draining their blood and bodily fluids.

"And those are the ones the length of your arm.

"You ask why there might be more. I say: why not? When does nature make just one of anything?"

"Assuming nature did this," Truman said.

I had the floor but Diane was looking daggers at me. Fredriche found his voice:

"Doctor Snow is correct. I have been sitting here trying to understand what the exponential change in physiological scale would mean; if nothing else they'd require enormous amounts of food.

"They eat after they spawn, which was only a month back. But what would be big enough for this *Petromyzon marinus* to eat?

"Lake Sturgeon and large Carp…"

One of the police officers laid his phone down on the table top.

"Sorry to interrupt the science lesson - I'm Sergeant Tran from the Ontario Provincial Police - I have a buddy who works for the Great Lakes Fishery Commission. I just rang him up. He told me they are investigating a sudden catastrophic fall in Sturgeon and Carp populations."

We sat in silence again; this time Fredriche blessed us with another of his catchy restatements of what we were thinking: "Oh, shit."

2100 hours

Somewhere on Lake Ontario...

I don't like cruises. Period.
My biggest nightmare is being stuck on a boat.
Joe Flanigan

The spray nailed me five minutes after the vessel hit full cruising speed. It was a warm evening; I wouldn't get chilled but regretted leaving my sports bra at home. I looked like a refugee from a wet sweatshirt contest.

The Coast Guard crew, focused on the tasks at hand, paid no attention. We were on a monster hunt.

By the end of the Queens conference everyone had established their role.

Lieutenant-commander Lesage and Captain Vukcic were in charge of protection on the high seas, while Sergeant Tran spearheaded a police task force involving the Ontario Provincial Police, Royal Canadian Mounted Police and Kingston Police Force.

Truman oversaw the task force, the Fisheries and Great Lakes Commission, and shadowy government figures.

Towards the end of the meeting Mr. Smith had silently entered the conference room and sat beside him.

He whispered into Truman's ear. They appeared to know each other.

"This is Mr. Smith with United States Homeland Security." That was all he said.

I began to wonder who Truman was in the government.

Diane had spoken for the scientists; she would liaise with the task force and explain the science.

Fredriche was headed back to the lab, tasked with reviewing witness statements, cell phone videos, and creating a "profile" of the lake monster.

And Diane announced that, given the presence of a bloodthirsty waterborne hell monster, the task force would embed a scientist. When eyes turned my way, I realized she meant me.

She placed me in charge of the "field work". Hence my presence on the *LaSalle*.

I don't mind boats but this one was going twenty-two knots over choppy water. Vukcic stood port side; I manned the starboard.

A fishing boat had spotted an overturned sailboat and called it in. We were on our way to investigate; scanning the water before us. The fishing boat had been asked to leave its location coordinates then take off.

As we approached the site we slowed and stopped.

Nothing; silence and a few circling birds. We were ten kilometres out and in the waning light there was nothing… I heard Vukcic call.

"Courtney, c'mere."

Making my way to the port side, I found the skipper calling down to the engineer.

"Martha; keep the engine running; I don't like it here. If we don't find anything, head straight back."

"Aye sir."

"Something feels wrong, Courtney; it's just a feeling, but those fishermen sounded spooked when they called."

As he spoke I looked up towards the bow; a naked woman sat with her legs dangling over the hull. She held her hand over her brow in a focused gaze.

"Do you see anything straight ahead?" I asked.

He looked towards the woman.

"No, I think we should take binoculars up there."

"I'll go," I said. "Oh, I have a funny habit of talking to myself, so don't worry if I look silly."

"No worries; do the same thing myself. Be careful; I don't want to be pulling you out of the drink."

A moment later I sat beside the woman and said - still casual: "How's everything?"

"Where did everyone go?" she asked.

"Who was with you?"

"Well, my husband, and another couple - we're swingers and we come out here to…"

"What happened?" I interrupted before she could elaborate.

"We were on deck and there was a huge thump underneath us. Jack - that's my husband's friend - flew right off me and into the water. I sat up to look and bam! It happened again. This time I flew into the water. See there I am!

A spectral finger pointed about twenty degrees to starboard. I could just make out something floating….

"Oh, wow - a beautiful light; and there's mom and dad…"

That bloody light! How was I ever going to ask proper questions if the dead kept fucking off into eternal peace?

"Captain!" I shouted back. He was watching me; either to determine if I was weird as I sounded, or to make sure I stayed onboard. "There's something up there." Now I pointed.

He shouted to the engineer and the other crew members came up top.

"You might as well go into the light while it's waiting," I said to her. "Thanks, enjoy eternity."

She vanished by the time Vukcic joined me.

At first we could barely make out the debris; the light was failing as the evening encroached. Then we could.

It looked like someone had chummed the water with a butcher's waste pile. These people had been torn to shreds.

One of the crew - Baker - joined us, and a moment later was puking over the side.

"Baker, back to work!" Vukcic shouted. "Damn you, the sun's almost down; I need spotlights and flashlights. Let's see what we can recover. Get crewman Vandenberg up here. Snap to it."

Vukcic was young to be a Captain; not much older than me, but he had the right stuff. I found out later that he commanded an offshore patrol vessel in the coastal fleet but for some reason had voluntarily returned to Kingston.

He was also, I noticed for the first time, kind of hunky.

Vandenberg was flat as clam; a better choice for the task at hand than poor Baker.

"Courtney, I need you," Vukcic said. "Take your binoculars and scan to the bow. I'll get Baker to watch to the stern." He looked around anxiously. "That fucking snake may still be around here somewhere."

I hadn't thought of that. My head popped up, ready to obey his order. But he was already yelling down to the engineer.

"Martha, call in our coordinates and findings. Keep the engine running. We may need to haul ass on short notice."

While Vukcic and Vandenberg did their grisly work, I scanned the horizon. The spotlights and flashlights over the inky chop were disorienting. Flashes of light and bloody chunks of dead swinger kept breaking my concentration.

When the first hump appeared - maybe fifty metres away - I almost missed it. But there was no mistaking the sinuous movement. It appeared then disappeared.

I punched the Captain hard on his shoulder and pointed. He didn't hesitate.

"Everyone below!" he bellowed, "Spatafora, the minute we're all down, gun it."

We lost precious moments storing guts. Vukcic was the last below. A massive grotesque head emerged from the deep; writhing, sleek and soundless.

"Go, go, go!" he yelled, and turned to me:

"We're gonna need a bigger boat!"

He didn't have a clue why I laughed.

Martha Spatafora punched the throttle and we took off. The *Lasalle* was a fast ship; twenty-five knots at full throttle. And our driver was determined to get every knot.

But the creature stayed metres behind the ship.

"Lampreys are one of the most efficient swimmers in the water," I shouted to no one in particular. "I have no idea how fast one this size can go."

"Vandenberg, keep an eye to stern." But Vandenberg didn't need orders.

"It's keeping up, sir," he said, "we're not gaining." The engine roared and strained under the sustained speed.

"We need more speed, Spatafora."

"I'm givin' her all she's got, Captain!"

I laughed again.

"Damn you, stop laughing, Snow."

Wow, no irony on the bridge. But the truth was I was the only one with the luxury to laugh. Out of nowhere, another order blared over the radio.

"This is United States Navy Commander Elias Brennan, break hard to starboard stat!"

Vukcic nodded curtly, and Spatafora hit the wheel. At twenty-five knots we nearly tipped.

All hell broke loose.

Two helicopters - as I had never seen them before - rained fire on the lake behind us. Over all the engines we could hear the buzz of their cannons and the explosions of air to sea missiles.

The dark sky glowed red.

Monday, July 10
Courtney's apartment

*His head was pounding and his vision skewed
in some way and he was vaguely amazed at
being alive and not sure it was worth it.*
Cormac McCarthy

I slept until ten am. I would have kept sleeping, but my phone rang.

After we reached shore; I called Brittany.

"Courtney, I've been scared shitless. Are you okay?"

"Did someone tell you what happened?"

"No, I told you; I know stuff and I know you were in danger. Are you okay?"

"I'm out of danger now but fucking traumatized; you would not believe…" I paused.

"Fredriche told me that bitch put you in charge of field work".

"Yeah, she did. That's what I was doing tonight - fucking field work. Listen, tell Fredriche to expect me late tomorrow. I'll be there but not right at nine."

"Sure, please Courtney - go home, drink some hot tea with lots of milk and sugar, then take something if you have it and go to bed!"

"Thanks."

The tea helped.

I thought I'd go to bed then but instead put on a Metallica album, headphones, and drank a half a bottle of vodka.

That helped too.

The call was strange.

"Hey girlfriend, wanna do coffee this morning?"

I couldn't place the voice. But she wasn't done:

"Why don't we meet at Coffee and Company at 11?"

"Ah, who is this?"

"Oh c'mon girlfriend; it's Marie, see ya there." She hung up

Coffee and Company
Downtown Kingston

*Good communication is just as stimulating
as black coffee, and just as hard to sleep after.*
Anne Morrow Lindbergh

Coffee and Company is a pleasant, brick and brown coffee shop in downtown Kingston. She was waiting, and waved when I stepped in the door. I grabbed a dark roast and joined her at the table.

"You don't strike me as the "hey girlfriend!" type."

"I never had the chance; I started as a young teen in Sea Cadets, moved on to the Royal Military College and then the Navy."

Lieutenant-commander Marie Lesage wore yoga pants with a long pink Nickelback t-shirt; likely her idea of casual wear. She sat straight in her chair and looked in my eyes as she spoke.

"I have women friends, but never had much of a youth."

"Why are we here? I need a coffee, but why like this?"

"We need to be discreet; there are things you and I need to discuss."

"Something important? Someone might hear us."

"Don't worry. There's no one close." I leaned down to whisper but looked over the room. Every table around us was occupied by men; handsome fit looking dudes with beards.

"Are they...?"

"They work for the same people as me. You and I are the two safest women in Kingston right now. The least of them could snap your neck without drawing a breath."

That didn't make me feel safer.

She changed the topic. "You had some excitement last night."

"That's one way of putting it. Are you referring to the monster that nearly ate us, or the helicopters that nearly blew us to pieces?"

"Bell AH-1 Super Cobras. Pretty hot machines, eh? Scare the shit out of the enemy."

"Uh huh. Well they fucking terrified me - and I'm friendly. Is that what you wanted to talk about?"

"No, we need to discuss some problems." I took a sip of my coffee, black and hot.

"Go on."

"Your colleagues are idiots." She held up a hand. "Please, I don't need you to tell me anything but it's obvious that Messi is smart but a stoner, and that *Doctor* Naylor is a bureaucrat who plagiarized her last paper."

"She did what? How do you know?"

"Our sources.

"And you, Courtney Snow, are a medium." I felt blood running to my face. I tried to cover by taking another swallow of coffee.

Marie Lesage was a striking woman with a strong lithe body and piercing brown eyes. I enjoyed her company but, like Truman, there was more to her than met the eye.

She tried to reassure me. "It's okay. We don't think you are crazy. Quite the contrary; you are the sharpest scientist onboard, and last night you used your gift to find the wrecked sailboat."

"How do you…"

"I know you are a medium and told Vukcic you might talk to yourself on the ship. Did you think Navy types just played with weapons, boats and tech?"

"Yeah, I kinda did…"

"Who did you see?"

"I didn't get her name. She was one of the dead and pointed out the wreck before she left."

"Want another coffee?"

"No thanks. So is that the problem - my colleagues aren't up to the task?"

"No, there's more. Last night, after you left, we and the Americans both sent vessels to the site. Guess what we found?"

"A few tons of shredded fish stock?"

"Nothing. Not a damn thing."

"Come on… Marie, you weren't there. There should be lamprey meat everywhere; the pieces left shouldn't be too big for this coffee cup."

"It got away."

"That's impossible."

"The air crew still don't believe it."

We sat in silence for a minute. The shop was full but around us, handsome young men were chattering in English and French, and somehow blending into the crowd.

"Crowds are anonymous," Marie said, reading my mind before she continued.

"So here's our problem. The Americans outgun us in every conceivable way but these are our waters. The word from on high is that this is a Canadian problem. Canadians need to solve it."

"That eel could cross the lake and be in Oswego by lunch," I said. "Then the Americans are going to very much consider it their problem."

"Which is one more reason we need a solution." So this was political. I shrugged.

"News of our eel is out, and the Prime Minister's Office will deliver a press release later today saying that a single creature is loose, its size is exaggerated and we should have it in hand by Saturday."

"Saturday! It's Monday now! What do you want me to do?"

"Be innovative, Courtney. Read Doctor Messi's profile and get back to me. There's a reason it was able to elude the guns last night and I want to know what it is."

Then, the kicker: "Talk to some dead people".

I didn't believe my ears.

"Say that again." She smiled and made eye contact. She had beautiful brown, and now I could see, cruel eyes.

"I want you to enlist the legion of the dead." I sat back in my chair. Seriously? I needed to put her in the picture.

"The legion of the dead are clueless oddballs; they walk around lost, preoccupied with dead people stuff."

"It's worked for us before." I looked up. She didn't seem to be joking.

"You use mediums?"

"You'd be surprised what we use. Now, we'll meet again tomorrow. Don't drink as much tonight."

"How do you...?" But she was already up and walking towards the door. Moments later, in staggered pairs, the men followed.

Last to leave, I started back towards the Ichthyology lab. Tourists, focused on the downtown core, crowded the streets of Kingston. I needed time to process, but I also needed to find Fredriche.

He sat in front of a computer in the wet room but he didn't appear to be working. Maybe he needed the fish to create a white background noise.

"This is too much pressure, Courtney," he said as I entered. "I can't handle it."

He couldn't handle it! Had Brittany told him about *my* night? But he was right; the expectations lay on him.

"So what does a huge *Petromyzon marinus* do that the little ones don't?"

"I've been going over the data for extinct primitive megafauna - and the extinction events themselves. So far as we understand, a big lamprey will behave like a little one. But here's the part that troubles me:

"We don't yet know how many there are. If there is already a catastrophic drop in *Cyprinids carpi* and *Acipenser fulvescens* and if humans stay out of the water they will run out of food. And what happens then?"

The professor was asking a question. I knew the answer.

"They migrate."

"Exactly - they'll start by colonizing the St. Lawrence Seaway, then say goodbye to whales and all living oceanic megafauna. It will unhinge the ecology of the earth. This could be our extinction event.

I felt a chill creeping up my spine; the hangover wasn't helping, but this was all too weird.

"There's not much time."

"I have another idea but I'm going to need you back at the lab to help me."

"Okay, I need to step away, Fredriche, but I will be back later this afternoon and do an evening shift with you."

Lemoine Point

It occurred to me that if I were a ghost, this ambience was what I would miss the most: the ordinary, day to day bustle of the living. Ghosts long, I'm sure, for the stupidest, unremarkable things.
Banana Yoshimoto

"Legion of the dead? You must be joking. This is the Navy? Wow, things have changed since my day." Nick Herkimer sat beside me on an isolated bench in the conservation area.

Then: "You saw a naked dead lady? Wow, she'd liven things up around here!"

I hoped that here no one would notice me talking to myself. A warm breeze played against my face, and birds artlessly sang their praises to Mother Earth.

"I need you, Nick." I had told him the whole story. I don't know why. When Commander Lesage called for the legion of the dead I'm not sure she meant a horny deceased farmer stuck in the woods.

He felt safe, somehow; clearly intelligent, he'd been around for a while and I needed to step outside the box.

"This has happened before," he said.

"What has?"

"Serpentine lake monsters. They named the last one Kingstie."

"What?"

"Google it."

"What do you know about googling anything?"

"I spend my days, eavesdropping, looking over shoulders and indulging my curiosity in any way you can imagine."

For the first time I was glad I saw ghosts; they were more legions of creepy voyeurs. That was probably why Marie enlisted them as spies.

"Courtney, lake monsters have appeared as long as human beings lived by the lake. Sure, some sighting were the imaginary products of too much grog, but not all of them. The accounts have been consistent over the years."

"You ever see one?"

"Once, in 1833, couple hundred ells out on the water. It resembled a water snake but much bigger. It rolled up to the surface then disappeared."

"You haven't seen this one?"

"No, but I know someone who might."

I felt a little trepidation as we walked towards the water and Nick wasn't doing a great job of reassuring me:

"Yeah, Lemoine has been drunk and looking out of the water for 145 years. You think I'm bad? If old Billy saw a naked chick on a boat you'd find out the real meaning of Lemoine Point!"

We found him.

Even on a hot afternoon he'd dressed for icy winter squalls. He stood on a flat rock by a rocky promontory looking out, wearing a heavy wool capote, a long muffler and a blue toque. He swayed on his pins, even in the gentle breeze.

"Hey Bill," Nick called out, "someone's here to visit you."

"Not now, Nick, I'm looking for my sled."

Nick rolled his eyes.

A couple paddled by in a canoe; they waved; Nick and Bill waved back. The paddlers only saw me.

"Bill, ya dim bastard; here's a comely wench!"

That did it; Lemoine swiveled so quickly he almost fell in the water. In a quick aside Nick said: "Sorry. I understand you reject the objectification of female sexuality, but it's the only thing outside of cheap whiskey that'll get his attention."

Lemoine rubbed his hands together when he laid eyes on me.

"Well. Lookee here! What have we?"

Once more I remembered Marie's legion of the dead; all I could muster was a gaggle of park-bound perverts.

"Don't be a boor, Bill; she can hear and see us." That helped. Lemoine straightened, took a pull from a ghastly bottle and replied formally.

"Good afternoon, young lady. I am the owner of this land..."

"It was mine first," Nick muttered.

"Pay no attention to him Miss...."

"Courtney... Miss Courtney."

"A delight to meet you Miss Courtney. I am Captain William Lemoine. How may I be of service? Be brief; I must return to my observations." He took another pull from the bottle. Was it always full? How did that even happen?

"Have you seen a lake monster?"

"Many times. I remember..."

"Recently; within the last few weeks..."

"It's all the same to me. Two weeks; a hundred years..."

"It would be like an eel."

"Ah yes, we used to pickle them - army rations. How the men complained on eel night!"

He turned as a pair of mallards flew past and looked out over the lake. I thought he had dismissed me. But he was pointing towards the distant shore.

"They came from…. there; they traversed the lake from that river mouth, and submerged one cables length to the west of this point."

"How fast were they travelling?"

"With great dispatch; perhaps twenty knots."

Lemoine said no more, and never even turned around. I reflected later that he at least knew how to act like a ghost.

"Wow, great intel - coolness!" Nick said.

"I kind of like the way *he* talks; you sound more out of date than Lemoine does."

This offended Nick. "I try to stay chill with the idiom and vernacular of the day."

We climbed the short promontory and followed the trail, through twittering birds and chubby begging squirrels, back to my car.

It was a lovely day and dated slang or not; I found Herkimer companionable. He looked ridiculous but he was quick and insightful.

Today was beautiful, though I wondered about the long rainy days where he walked alone in the woods. This was a man who enjoyed gregarious activity.

"Lemoine's intel should give us a trajectory to the spawning grounds," he said. "You're the scientist but it sounds important."

"It's very important," I said. "I need to get back and report this."

"Sorry you have to leave so soon." He sounded like he meant it.

"Are you always stuck here, Nick? Can you leave?"

"I can accompany a person - haunt them," he said tentatively. "Haven't left the park for many years; Maracle took me to the reservation once. A few of the elders were mediums; should have seen them jump!"

He spoke as if terrifying old people was the funniest thing.

"Why don't you come with me to town?"

"I wouldn't ask that of you, Courtney but thank you for the offer. It is greatly appreciated." For a moment the look of sadness returned. "I'd be underfoot; do you want me following you everywhere and hanging around your pad?"

No, I didn't.

"Well, someday we'll go on an outing; take in a movie or something."

"That sounds like fun; it would be like a date."

No, but it might liven life up for him; give him a respite from the leafy pathways.

I drove back to Queens, thinking about one word Lemoine had uttered: "they".

Ichthyology Lab
Queens University

Fredriche was only a little stoned; under this kind of pressure we were lucky he wasn't falling over. But it worried me. He had fixed himself in front of the computer; papers lay everywhere.

"I haven't slept," he said. "I am trying to generate behavioral models for our fish. But I need more data."

"I found a witness who saw two of the lampreys off Lemoine Point. He wasn't clear on the time but I have a speed, location and trajectory."

"Excellent! I'll pull up the maps and maybe we can figure out where they spawned. Grab a seat; I'll just run to the men's…"

He came back shortly, just a little more baked.

Courtney's Apartment

We like the wrong sorts of girls, they wrote.
They are usually the ones worth writing about.
Catherynne M. Valente

By nine I was clad in pyjamas, sitting in front of the news, clutching a cup of Earl Grey tea. My apartment, looking down on Princess Street, seemed quiet. I should have cherished that sensation but didn't.

I had muted the television at some point and sat dissociated. When my thoughts came into focus, I realized that they were erotic and featured Phil Vukcic - no surprise there, and...Nick.

I didn't even know if Phil had someone in his life; I had barely spoken to him. As for Nick - no future there. But... he was emerging as amusing, and kind of a gentleman.

The dead were typically batty or angry but Nick seemed devoid of malice or bitterness. He just wanted to chat and enjoy himself.

A sharp rap on the door interrupted my reverie. Behind it stood Marie Lesage.

"Hey girlfriend! I came over and brought us a treat!"

Though on the short side; of hair and body; she had a strong physical presence. Those deep brown eyes should have unbalanced her look but they seemed to root it.

The treat had been contained in a brown paper bag.

"Wine?"

"No, over-proof rum; picked it up at a layover in Jamaica. Can you find us a couple of tumblers?"

"What are we going to put in the rum?" She stared at me blankly. I tried something else.

"You told me not to drink tonight."

"You believed a sailor who told you not to drink?"

I gave up and obediently fetched glasses and emptied a tray of ice into a bowl. I wasn't going to approach that stuff straight up.

"Pussy," she said, pouring herself a straight shot. She then sat on my sofa and crossed two strong looking legs.

"You've spent a lot of time playing with boys, haven't you?"

She looked sheepish.

"That's the navy for you." She leaned forward and looked intently into my eyes. "But I like playing with girls too…"

When I giggled, she turned her gaze inward for a moment… "Oh, oh, I didn't mean it like that, I like guys…"

Now I laughed out loud.

"You can play with whoever you want, sailor girl. I'm the one here who plays with eels for a living." I took a pull of my drink and winced. In the glass it looked like dirty ice tea. "Whoa, strong but (cough) smooth."

"Next time I'll bring pink champagne."

"I would pay good money to watch you drink it."

It was time to shift away from the oddball chatter.

"I met with the legion of the dead today."

"I know; we saw you walking around Lemoine Point talking to yourself." I paused to take that in, then another swallow.

"Well, what did the dead have to say?"

I told her.

"So there are more than one; probably more than two. How do we take the fuckers out?" I shrugged.

"That's the problem. Lampricides have been reasonably successful in controlling the population. But even with the little ones we have concerns about the effect of chemical warfare on the larger ecosystem.

"Anything strong enough to kill these creatures would probably destroy all life in Lake Ontario."

Marie took another pull on her rum. She drank it like water. I was already feeling the effects.

"How's your boss coming with his profile?"

"It should be ready shortly." I didn't know Fredriche that well. And I didn't know how people perceived him, but we would all need to have confidence in his work.

"He comes across as a flake," I said, "but he earned his reputation. He is a bright man."

I enjoyed Marie's company but also felt antsy. I glanced around the apartment. It looked like the flop of an itinerant student. Much of my stuff sat unpacked in boxes. A painters' drop cloth had been enlisted as a curtain.

I possessed a fancy degree but that was it; in most ways I didn't differ from an undergraduate. My adult life had never really begun.

"I feel the same way," she said. "Every year, I studied all the time, except for summer when I was off training. I'm a young Lieutenant-commander but all I have ever done is train and work."

How come everyone knew what I was thinking? Did she have the place bugged? Maybe she was just Sherlocking me. She definitely out-drank me.

"Does that make us pathetic?"

"I don't feel pathetic. I feel like getting drunk. And dancing."

The evening quickly devolved into alcohol and hilarity. We put on a Nirvana CD and danced around the room. We smoked the two old reefers I kept in my desk drawer.

Later we played forties music and danced cheek to cheek.

We joked about the cute boys; the Special Forces guys, Truman, and especially the studly Coast Guard Captain Vukcic.

Or maybe that was more me.

I told her ghost stories and she told me… not much; she said if she told me anything interesting, she'd have to kill me.

Even though I found her adorable, she was also a dangerous loon.

We danced around until a pleasant young officer from the Kingston Police arrived at the door, responding to a noise complaint.

Marie batted her eyes at him unconvincingly, then ordered him to "stand down, sailor".

I turned off the music.

She smiled, hugged me and walk out the door with the cop.

I passed out.

Tuesday, July 11
Bay of Quinte

The fishing was good, it was the catching that was bad.
A.K. Best

"This is what they call fake news. Mark my words; the government wants to neutralize fishermen. They know we are the last independent thinkers."

"Kyle, they say it's unsafe to be on the water right now."

"This is a big boat; nothing smaller than a whale is going to hurt us. Please try to relax. Crack another beer. We have the Bay and the fish to ourselves. If I can get the sonar working, we'll catch our limit."

Kip McLean was the last guy on the hockey team who still went fishing with Kyle Gifford. Kyle could find fish but the incessant stream of bitter political rambling grew old quickly.

Mind you, Kip thought to himself, he had a point. The papers were keeping things dark. Accurate news was difficult to find - even on Twitter. All anyone knew was that some snot-nosed Queens kid had been attacked in the water.

The rest was bullshit rumours; helicopters, shots in the night. Probably reported by lefty stoners with conspiracy theories.

"Assad's behind this," Kyle said.

Kip had to think for a moment.

"What does, ah, Syria want with Lake Ontario?" As soon as the words were out of his mouth, he regretted them; he should have been pouring beer in, not stupid questions out.

"Well, it's like this. Syria - and Russia and Iraq and ISIS, are looking for a distraction right now…"

Kip sighed, took a drink and waited. They should be trolling open water. What was the problem with the damned sonar?

"C'mere Kip, check this out." Kip obediently stood up and walked over to the sonar. He could see the green power light, but the screen showed nothing but a few squiggles.

"Have you fucked with the controls?"

"Of course. Look at this. The depth is 20 feet. We are in at least 90 feet of water right now. How come it says 20?"

Kip shrugged. That was weird. He pointed to the screen.

"It says 17 now." They reflexively looked up. The water lay still on a Thursday morning. Were they drifting? "Is there a rock or a shoal here, Kyle?"

"No, for crying out loud; we are in deep water; there are no rocks or shoals… shit, Kip it says 10 feet…"

"Get the fuck out of here." Kyle was already at the throttle. He shoved it forward and they both heard the engine roar.

For a moment they didn't move as a half million dollar fishing cruiser ascended from the water's surface and the propeller bit into the flesh of a monster.

Like an enraged bronco, the lamprey bucked backwards, throwing the boat through the air, landing top down in 90 feet of water. Kyle died on impact. Kip lived long enough to feel the pull of the giant sucking mouth…

Portsmouth Olympic Harbour

My Mom said she learning how to swim when someone took her out on the lake and threw her off the boat. I said, "Mom, they weren't teaching you how to swim."
Paula Poundstone

I was hung over but one glance at Phil Vukcic's grim visage stilled any wish to joke about it.

I wasn't sure why Diane called and told me to get right to Portsmouth harbour, but I could see the urgency in everyone's face.

"Get on," he said tersely. He was looking very handsome in his uniform. I wondered how much Marie remembered of my mooning over him last night.

He shouted down to Spatafora and Vandenberg. He was always shouting at someone. Then he called to Baker to release the rope. The moment I had both feet on the deck he yelled: "Go."

As she navigated the vessel around the jetty and through the yachts and million dollar sailboats, he took my arm and briefed me.

His hand generated warmth and strength... but he brought me back to reality.

"Two fishermen are missing. We believe their boat's overturned near the Lafarge Cement Plant. Someone spotted at least two large serpentine creatures around the wreck.

"They're sending in the Cyclones to hose down anything alive and bigger than a human being, then they're going to launch anti-submarine Mark 46 torpedoes. Our job is to run in full speed, check for any survivors the Navy helos missed, then fuck off and outrun the lampreys before they shoot."

"Then we go back and obtain samples of whatever's left of the eels. This is going to be dangerous, Courtney."

"No fucking shit, Phil! Are you fucking insane!"

"I'm only taking *you* under orders, Courtney. I refused, told them I wasn't putting a civilian in harm's way, but Dr. Naylor approached Truman and insisted a scientist be present.

"Now get below and stay the hell out of my way."

Every time I had seen Vukcic he'd been the epitome of warm professionalism. But today he was wired. He clearly thought this mission was crazy, and worried more about the crew than himself.

My job was sit, out of the way, until fish parts became available. I resolved to spend the time thinking of ways - should I make it back - of feeding Diane to those slimy fuckers.

I nearly fell over the side when my phone beeped with a text.

Hey girlfriend. I'm in charge of the Air Cav. Vukcic and I tried to keep you out of this. That bitch you work 4 has too much pull. Told 'em I know a dead fish when I see one but no good.

Stay out of the fucking way while we blow the goddam thing to hell. Luv u, M

I thought about sending a snappy reply but she was busy. I felt like throwing my phone over the side just for the hell of it but it beeped again.

You are in real danger, Courtney. Fredriche is stoned, drunk and crying in the bedroom. He won't tell me what's going on but I can tell you - I've never intuited anything as strongly before - this is not going to end well. DO NOT GET ON THAT BOAT.

We were one hundred metres off shore and cruising at 25 knots for our destination. I was committed.

Gee thanks Brittany; nothing like a delay action psychic.

As the roar of the engine drowned my thoughts, I took deep breaths to pull myself together.

We saw the copters in the distance, hovering as we approached. Spatafora throttled down and the sudden silence was scarier than the race to the destination.

I followed Vukcic and Baker on deck. I was disobeying orders but I wanted - no, I needed to help out.

Vukcic had been trained to never take his vessel and crew into an unsafe situation. But rules were being broken today.

Terror enhanced my senses. I could hear the breeze and feel the sun on my shoulder. And the prickle of sweat starting down under my bra, which I had remembered to wear today.

I'd dressed in jeans and a Toronto Raptors tee; the only thing I could find on short notice. Between that and the life jacket I felt like a fucking idiot, surrounded by professionals.

We were about a hundred metres from the wreck now. The vessel gently rocked to the lapping of waves as we approached from the east.

It didn't see much; just a white hull bobbing in the water.

Martha Spatafora called: "Skip, Commander Lesage wants you on the radio."

"Okay, Trade places. I'll take the Conn while I talk to her. I need someone good spotting."

"Aye, sir."

They traded places. If Baker had any feelings about the "someone good" remark it didn't show. No room for injured emotion on the *LaSalle*.

Baker, followed by Vandenberg, headed to the stern to watch from there, while Martha and I looked over the bow rail.

Then she crossed herself and on a reverent note stated: "Madre Dio protega mi."

"I didn't see diddly-squat on sonar," she said after that, more to herself than to me. "This is vexing shit."

"You see anything?" We were within twenty feet of the other vessel, drifting.

"Lots of mud, weed, and some kind of viscous slime. The water's deep here; something's stirred up the whole bottom.

"Ah, fuck…" This was me. I didn't have a sailor's cachet for profanity but something bobbed to the surface. Something ugly, colourful and disfigured.

"Is that one of the fisherman?" Martha asked. She pulled me out of the way to get a better look.

"Hard to tell, it doesn't look like a fish…" I said, making a pathetic attempt to be relevant.

Martha stood up. "We better get this in; I'll get the net…"

"Spatafora!" Phil yelled. She rolled her eyes.

"He's starting to sound like my husband," she said with a chuckle.

"There's something wrong with the fucking sonar. It's … fucking hell…."

After, when I had time to think, I wondered if this was what running over an IED felt like. The deck beneath our feet just lifted, with the sickening sound of the crushing hull.

A scream came from the stern; the last anyone would hear from Baker.

I fell back flat; the wind knocked out of me. The vessel lurched to the portside. I grabbed a rail as we straightened.

Martha was out cold; blood was pouring onto the deck from her head. I pulled myself to my knees and reached for her.

I lifted from under her arms and began dragging her away from the bow.

Then I stopped.

That verminous face, dripping with oleaginous slime, layered in sharp spiralling tines, was silently emerging from the water.

Martha groaned. "We have to fight…"

It continued to rise like a cobra from the water. How the fuck did it do that? The face moved towards us. She gasped.

"…no guns on a Coast Guard vessel…"

She spoke too soon.

Captain Phil Vukcic emerged from below deck with a pump action shotgun. I guess there was a gun on this one.

He didn't waste time. Working the pump he pointed and shot. With a massive boom he scored a direct hit. Then another.

Walking calmly forward, he worked the pump again. The creature had recoiled, and exploded chunks of lamprey sashimi flew, but it didn't submerge. He raised the gun to his shoulder for a kill shot…

A second creature emerged from the starboard, grabbed him and disappeared.

The first monster stared at the bloody deck; I was now alone with the bleeding engineer. I tried to get off my knees and made it to my feet wobbling.

"Go fuck yourself," I screamed. "You fucking shit fish! I fucking hate you!"

It continued to rise even higher.

I suppose it's a measure of the modern age, but when my phone bleeped I looked:

It was that fucking rum-soaked Navy madwoman:

Duck

What! All hell breaking loose and she's birdwatching... oh...shit.

The opening riff to *Black Math* by *White Stripes* hit me like a hot wave as the Cyclones screamed in from the east, cannons blazing.

The lamprey disappeared as I keeled onto the breaking deck.

As the Apocalypse rained in bloody crimson spouts; a kind of calm overcame me. I hugged Martha Spatafora to my breast like a child, as we slipped under the cool waters, and into Poseidon's loving embrace.

Kingston General Hospital

*God has mercifully ordered that the human brain works
slowly. First the blow, hours later the bruise.*
Walter de la Mare

"Mom?"

A warm hand in mine; another stroking my brow.

"It's me, Courtney. You rest."

It wasn't my mom's voice. She died two years before, after
my father. I was returning to the room and felt strangely
peaceful. Brittany continued:

"You're okay. The doctor said nothing's broken or damaged.
We're here to keep you company."

My eyes opened. I saw her face and heard the hum of
the medical apparatus; my arm itched from the IV and
bandage on my forearm.

Two people sat silently at the back of the room. When
she saw me focus Marie Lesage winked one of those huge
brown eyes. Truman nodded.

I knew they'd drugged me as the memories returned. My
voice sounded sluggish and low.

"Baker, Vandenberg ... Phil?"

"They're gone," Brittany said. "I'm sorry."

"Martha?"

"She's okay. She has a concussion but her husband is with
her. You wouldn't let her go; the Navy divers had to pry
you two apart."

"The fish?" Marie stood and approached Brittany.

"She needs rest," she said.

I wanted to cry but I was too groggy. I fell asleep again.

I awoke again in the dark. They'd placed me in a private room. I looked around for a clock. It was 3 am. My bed lay by a large window overlooking the lake; I could see the dark waters lit by summer moonlight.

So peaceful. So serene.

1100 hours
Wednesday July 12
Sandy Island Beach State Park
Upstate New York

*She was starting to think that it might be fun
to be in control of the Universe*
Nicki Elson

Sandy Island Park bills itself as the only significant freshwater dune site in the northeastern US.

Today the beach was open but no one bathed in the water. The lifeguards warned against "environmental issues". Everyone who followed the internet knew the issue was a bloodthirsty sea-monster that - so far - confined itself to dining in Canada.

People grumbled but few ventured into the lake.

"The only significant freshwater *dude* site in northeastern US," Jackie Hansen said to himself. He and Sparkle were floating on small inflatable raft a hundred feet offshore. An anchor had been thrown and the small craft bobbed in the light waves.

Fiftyish, ponytailed, potbellied, topless; they gazed through polarized lenses up at the cerulean sky and passed an aromatic spliff back and forth; slowly, carefully.

"You worried about the sea snake?"

"It lives in Canada." Having located the beast to the Canadian side of the lake, Jackie took another toke.

"They've legalized weed there. Think it likes weed?" Sparkle was full of questions today.

"If they've legalized weed; we oughta' start paddling now; be there by tomorrow morning if we hurry!"

Neither of them were moving, let alone paddling or hurrying anywhere, so they lay back and chuckled.

It happened quickly but like Loch Ness in tourist season plenty of beach goers gazed out over the water. They weren't disappointed.

The serpentine body of the lamprey reared twenty feet out of the water. People screamed. Some reflexively pointed their phones.

"Something going on?" were the last words spoken by Sparkle - ever - as the monster simply fell on both of them. The ripping and sucking could be heard on the beach. People cried, retched and ran to their cars.

Thursday July 13
Queens Conference Center

Nothing in life is to be feared, it is only to be understood.
Now is the time to understand more, so we can fear less.
Marie Curie

Everyone stared at the video. It resembled a shaky cam horror movie. We were watching YouTube on a large screen.

"Too many people saw this," Truman said. "We are out of time."

Shivering in my chair, I sat quietly. I had a robust constitution but being present at all was an accomplishment. Some had resisted my return. Marie told me later of a fierce argument.

I had discharged myself from hospital, ignoring the objection of the attending physician. He told me to go straight home and get into bed.

I did - for an hour, then called Marie and told her I was ready. She said: "Fuck off and go back to bed." She hung up on me and called Truman.

Truman wanted me back. Marie was against it. They made a quick round of the committee. Fredriche, influenced by Brittany took a stand for once, and said he was against my return.

Diane cast the deciding vote. She said simply, "I want her back."

So here I was, arms folded across my chest; hurting.

Everything ached. My shoulders and hips throbbed, my skin prickled and burned, and my heart...

This was war, and I had to be tough. I always had to be tough, but I kept seeing Phil Vukcic on the deck with the shotgun. He went down fighting.

I would too.

I refused to be grateful to Diane but it was good that I had been on the vessel; good that Martha Spatafora had made it home to her family.

Our committee was complete. A Commander Kerr had taken Vukcics' place for the Canadian Coast Guard, which rattled me at first. But he had won me over by mouthing "thanks" across the table when no one else was looking.

Smith, the American, sat quietly beside Truman who now took charge.

"We need a plan to destroy these things now," he said. "I am open to ideas but let's hear from Doctor Messi. He's prepared a profile."

Fredriche looked up from his papers. He looked different; it took a moment, but I realized that he showed no sign of cannabis poisoning. He'd trimmed his beard, put on clean clothes and sat straight in his chair.

"As most of you know we killed one of the eels after the assault on the *LaSalle*. We were able to retrieve skin, nerve fibre and viscera. Doctor Naylor and I have been in the lab since then; virtually around the clock."

"We've missed Doctor Snow but colleagues from the biology department have helped in the testing.

"We were damn lucky to kill the one fish."

"Dead hit with a lot of ordnance," Marie said.

"An ordinary small lamprey is a miracle of nature. This thing is... enhanced. Even dissecting the skin; three members of the engineering department worked for hours to create something hot and sharp enough to penetrate the dermis.

"This fish is full of chemicals that don't belong in an eel. It's nervous system; well, I'm not sure it's even dead now. Then we observed something beyond our comprehension; even though we both witnessed it." Fredriche turned towards the screen at the front of the room.

"This is a short video of our attempt to x-ray one of the intact sections of the dead eel. Watch closely."

The team had placed the camera on a tripod and Fredriche was droning on about the projected location of this piece on the whole lamprey and angle of radiation to the dermis and as we leaned forward in our seats - the slimefish filet disappeared.

"Fuck me." Sergeant Tran spoke for all of us.

"Where is it?" I asked.

"It's still there." He resumed the playback. "This seems to be some kind of stealth eel. It reacts to radiation - and we think other things - by becoming invisible.

"It's not invulnerable; that's why we got one, but it's hard to kill and almost impossible to track."

We continued to watch the screen. A moment passed after Fredriche shut off the radiation and the fish chunk reappeared.

"So," Diane continued, "we had a big problem before, it's bigger now. There are American casualties. And our cousins to the south will not be patient."

Tran didn't look patient himself. He asked the obvious question: "So what's the plan?"

Fredriche looked up from his computer. I was amazed to see him like this. I knew he was bright, but he'd always played the role of dissolute stoner.

"We have three problems. One - how do we find the Lampreys? Two - how do we get them where we can take them out? Three - how do we kill them?

Smith cleared his throat. This caught us all off guard. We had become accustomed to him as a silent partner.

"If you can get them to one place - together - we'll take care of the rest."

This excited our imagination. What did the Americans have that could destroy these things? Did we want to know?

Tran, the practical cop, spoke again: "So Doctor Messi; how do we get them together?"

"We've had research on the go for years; that's why we brought Doctor Snow on board; it was the subject of her doctoral thesis and her current work. Courtney, can you explain?"

I nearly jumped in my seat. Oh, fuck, of course. This should have been obvious.

"Pheromones," I said. "We attract them sexually. 3kPZS can attract females from up to 2 kilometres. But... these fish are different..." I was thinking out loud now. All eyes were on me. "These are enhanced eels... they seem to be pack hunters...the males would follow... could work."

"It will work," Truman said, with more decision than the science warranted. "We don't have much time. The science team will prepare for the release of pheromones where... Doctor Messi?"

"We have identified from the movement vectors to the stream mouth where they spawned. If we release pheromones there, clear the area, and our behavioral models hold; we should be able to get them together.

"We could evacuate on a pretext; maybe an alleged car accident..."

"Happy to oblige," said Sergeant Tran.

"So if we know where and when the eels will appear we can now arrange for their sudden demise," Fredriche completed his thought.

"How are we going to release pheromones on that scale and all at once?" I too had practical questions.

"It can be done remotely," Diane said.

"Our equipment isn't that reliable," I said, "especially on this scale. Someone would need to be on the ground or in the water." I looked at Marie Lesage and Smith: "Who does that sort of thing - JTF 2... Navy SEALS?"

I looked to Marie and Smith, but Diane answered:

"Courtney, scientists do that sort of thing, and you are the specialist."

Every eye - again - swiveled towards me. I couldn't talk for a moment as the implications became clear.

"So a dozen or more horny and hideous monsters will be racing at lightning speed for - me - where they will be annihilated by a nightmarish hell weapon wielded by the US military?"

People nodded around the table.

"That's more or less how we saw it going," Truman said. "We like how you handled yourself on the *LaSalle*. You can manage in a crisis, and you are the right person for the job."

"Our weapons are precise," Smith said. "We should be able to take them out without hitting you." Truman resumed:

"Doctor Snow will leave with Commander Kerr and his crew for a reconnaissance of the stream mouth tomorrow at 0500. So I suggest we get going with our jobs."

Everyone stood to leave, except me who remained seated - and stunned. Marie looked back.

"You coming girlfriend? I want to take you home and tuck you in. Brittany Messi is there making soup or something. We'll need you rested up for tomorrow morning.

She drove me home.

"This plan is fucking insane," I noted to her. She looked like she hadn't a care in the world. The bitch was having fun.

"You have a better plan?"

"I could be killed; in fact I probably will be killed."

"I know, that's a responsibility I have to take. It's part of being an officer." Marie sighed.

Was that was her idea of consolation?

Marie dropped me at my apartment and Brittany was waiting. She gave me a long hug on arrival.

"The team appointed me official nurturing woman," she grumbled. "But I want to feed you and put you to bed anyway. These people are crazy as shithouse rats - right out of Dr. Strangelove. They told me they had an important job for you."

"The technical term for my job is 'target'." She took my hand and squeezed.

"Are you okay?"

I laughed. Then laughed again; then couldn't stop. I convulsed and became hysterical. I had never laughed like this before.

"I'm a fucking fish scientist working with eels in a lab. I went to school for thirty years and now I'm supposed to seduce a seething of homicidal lampreys or die trying."

"Eat your soup," Brittany said, "I used organic chicken with shallots." I shut up, took a deep breath and picked up a spoon.

Friday, July 14
Onboard Canadian Coast Guard Motor Launch George Brown
0530

We are imprisoned in the realm of life, like the sailor
on his tiny boat, on an infinite ocean.
Anna Freud

Captain Kerr conferred below with his engineer. Marie and Sergeant Tran were looking over their shoulder at the radar. We were on route to the stream mouth.

Already luminescent and warm; a beautiful day beckoned; the spray splashing my face felt cold and refreshing.

With everyone safely below, I made my way to the bow.

"Do you see the light?" I asked. Phil Vukcic smiled sadly.

"I'm ignoring it," he said. "I want to see this job through."

"How is it for you?" I asked. "Being dead."

"Ever spent a Sunday in Napanee?" Had Phil acquired a sense of humour in death?

He wasn't finished: "If I can help you Courtney, let me know."

"Thanks," I said. "I have to go." I could see Marie emerging from the cabin. She knew about the medium thing but I wanted Phil to myself.

She held a chart in her hand.

"We're almost there," she said. "What are we looking for?"

"Lampreys are picky about where they screw around with the other lampreys. They prefer a gravelly bottom in rapid water for their spawning beds, with muddy or sandy bottom in quiet water nearby, for the larvae.

"We had our own charts but found people from the geography department to go through them with us. I wanted to figure out where the channel emerged, the gradients, depth and especially any perennial shoals where I could set up the trap for release.

"Engineers are mechanizing the traps for much greater explosive release and the biochemists are trying to enhance the attraction to the olfaction glands. Shouldn't be needed with these super-fish but we want them to come running from anywhere in the lake."

"Timing will be important," Marie said. "We are going to need to know where you are after the pheromones are released so the Yanks don't hit you."

"I won't be getting very far away; what are they using that can miss me over a few dozen metres?"

"They won't tell us."

"So I release the trap, move out of the way, a dozen murderous, nearly impervious Petromyzontidae are whacked, and I'm just fine."

"I think so," Marie said, with little conviction.

"Why do I think I'm about to garnish the biggest bouillabaisse in history?"

Marie slapped me on the back. "You'll be fine, girlfriend. Whoops, we're slowing down, got to check in with Kerr."

"You get the short straw?" Phil had a straight face. He had drifted over and listened in on the conversation. He was a literal dude and I don't think he meant it as a joke. But who knew?

"Seems like it."

"It's a crappy plan, Courtney, be careful."

"Thanks." I always appreciated support from the dead.

By this point we had slowed to a crawl. I scanned the horizon. If I had to be offered as a sacrifice somewhere, this was it. I needed to confirm the structure but a deep channel, shallow shoal and long low grade to the channel was the best scenario for trapping the lampreys and my getting out intact.

Kerr came above deck and gave me a thumbs up.

"This is perfect Doctor Snow," he shouted. "We're confirming the depth and structure but everything seems to be where it's supposed to be. Nothing's shifted."

"Great, hold still and give me a few minutes…" I wore a long tee over my bathing suit. I lifted it over my head. Kerr turned away. I smiled. I only had to be hot to lady lampreys.

I put on the snorkel and fins I'd brought and dove. The cold water was bracing, but I focused on the underwater structure. I swam to the shoal, stood, measured the depth, and paddled over to the point where I could stand with my head and shoulders above water.

If I was doing this tomorrow, I was damn well going to rehearse ahead of time. I started to walk quickly towards shore, realized I had to lose the fins, flipped them off and kept going.

This would be slow with a few hundred tons of killer eels bearing down on me.

That completed, I swam back to the launch. Marie pulled me in.

"That's what I would have done," she said while pulling me on board.

"I have to get back to the lab," I said. "Let's get out of here."

Lemoine Point

I am concerned for the security of our great Nation; not so much so much for any threat from without, but because of the insidious forces working within.
Douglas MacArthur

Nick Herkimer

Summer is my favorite time of year. So many people wandering around; chatting, looking at their phones and tablets. I learn so much.

This summer felt better than most. Over the years I've had so few people to talk to; and it had been sixty or seventy years since I had talked with a woman.

Courtney reminded me of Charlotte; smart and strong willed. As I walked under the tree shadows, my thoughts were warm and elegiac. I even sighed.

I'm a voyeur but what choice do I have? The late Mister Johan Nicholas Herkimer can't walk up and introduce himself to a new friend. And if I ever stop listening, I'll end up like that mad bastard Lemoine; staring out to sea and muttering to himself.

I enjoy conspiracies; some people walk and talk and plot. I can spot them from a mile away. Sometimes it's romantic; sometimes it's something darker.

There have been murders planned; they saddened me because someone murdered me and doomed to me to henceforth wander these paths. But no use feeling sorry for yourself!

I knew this couple were up to no good. Their body language wasn't sexual but they were close together. They were dressed for work, suits etc., unusual for this park.

87

Didn't like the look of her; all frowns and severe angles. Him - for reasons I couldn't place, I loathed. He reminded me of someone...

Mighty Jehoshaphat - he looked like Moses Rogers! The son of a bitch who killed me. Of course, the American accent... I knew it.

My first thought: the bastard was formulating a plot against a workmate; taking out an office rival. And in a way, I was right.

I fell in beside them and tuned in, with eavesdropping skills honed over two hundred years.

"She has to go," said the woman.

"Why?" said the man.

One of the lampreys needs to escape so we can use it for our own purposes. She'll figure out why - unless she is the casualty of the escape.

Lampreys? Holy Hannah; this concerned Courtney.

"I've never liked her and hoped she'd go down on that Coast Guard boat with the rest of the crew. Instead, she's still with us."

"Okay," the man said, "I'm sold - what do we do?"

"The plan's set for tomorrow. Courtney will be ready to release the pheromones and your weapons will be in position."

"Yes, that's right."

"The lampreys will be drawn to the 3kPZS, but they also react to sound and movement. I have put a small sonic generator in the remote she'll be using. At least one of the lampreys will respond to it and then its lights out Doctor Snow."

"How do we activate it?"

"We can do that from shore; we'll go as observers, easy-peasy."

They were trying to kill Courtney! I had to act. But what the hell could I do?

"Tonight at 1900 hours we're meeting to complete the plan and review the equipment. I will confirm the arrangements. What are you going to do?"

"I'll make a fuss about not hitting the girl with the weapons. We'll also tell her to stay still during the attack. If one veers off from the other the weapons crew will ordered not to kill that eel. From there we'll set up an electronic containment field from the sub and reel it in."

"The sub?"

"You think we don't have one nearby? This is organic matter with the gift of invisibility - right on our doorstep. We're going to catch it, weaponize it and put it back in the field."

"Rogers, you are a piece of work."

"Likewise Doctor Naylor. But don't use my name anywhere around here; it's Smith to everyone."

He had an ulterior motive, and she was a spy. Wow, his great great granddaddy was a prick and so was he. This time he wasn't getting away with it.

I made a decision on the spot to attend that meeting and tell Courtney. I had to haunt one of them.

Figuring Diane more likely to see Courtney, I haunted her.

It's not difficult. You step inside them for a moment and, voila, you're attached. You step out again, and go where they go.

Doctor Naylor shivered as I stepped out.

"Brrr, did you feel a chill?"

"No, now go back to the lab and make sure everything goes the way it's supposed to. Tomorrow night I want the girl dead and a lamprey in custody."

We continued to stroll down the path to the parking lot. While I was haunting her I could perform a few minor stunts; screw with electricity a little, push items off tables and the like.

I hadn't haunted anyone since old Maracle took me on a day trip to a bar downtown in the sixties. I couldn't drink but he enjoyed the company.

Indian hating ruffians came by and started giving him a hard time. Then I gave them a hard time. Lights flashed, beer bottles danced on the table; I even made a radio go on right beside one of them. He turned so fast he hit it with his head.

I can still see them running down Princess Street.

Good times! But no stunts for me today. I had to get close enough to Courtney to warn her.

We left in separate cars; Rogers in one, and Doctor Naylor and I in the other.

Queens University

*If you know the enemy and know yourself you need not fear
the results of a hundred battles*
Sun Tzu

Nick Herkimer

What a long afternoon that was! I hadn't spent the day with
a chick since the First World War; and even then we just
chatted about her husband in the army and she drank tea.

I won't get into Doctor Naylor's creepy grooming habits
but I discovered why she hated Courtney so much.

Looking over her shoulder while she skyped I discovered
a lover; maybe half her age. He was also a post doc in
ichthyology.

"Hey lover, I have something good to tell you."

*"Hey Baby, I miss the cuddling and sweet talk. I want to show you
my slippery eel again"*

Oh yuk!

*"That post doc position with Messi. It's going to come open again
shortly. This is our chance to be together."*

"Wow, that's great Diane. What happened to Snow?"

*"Nothing - yet. I can't talk about it but maybe you can polish up
your resume and sometime soon I'll make that eel slippery for you."*

For a moment I considered un-haunting her and heading
back to the park. Anything would be better than having
to listen to this. But I couldn't let Courtney down.

When that pestiferous chat was complete she dressed for
the meeting and we left for Queens.

Rogers/Smith met her at the door. He was in a hurry.

"Don't go in Diane. I need you to go scout our spot for tomorrow. Sorry, but we can't risk them finding something else for you for do. We have to be close enough for our remote control to work."

She glanced at the door. I looked inside. There was Courtney. I waved. I jumped and I shouted but she was deep in conversation with a foxy babe in a uniform.

Then Diane pulled away and I was yanked along. I guess I was going along for this scouting expedition then - well, I'd better think of something...

Saturday, July 14
Lemoine Point

Trust is as slippery as a basket of eels sometimes.
Robert Jordan

Lampreys play at night. Marie called me early and told me to sleep in; changes were being made at the U.S. end and we were going operational at dusk, not dawn.

Sleep in on the day of my probable death? Not likely; I decided to go for a walk in the woods. A few hours remained before our pre-mission check in, so I drove to Lemoine Point.

I wanted to talk to Nick. His cheery banter provided a welcome respite from fish-talk, and pestilent planetary threats.

I remembered his hangouts and wandered about looking for him. Another enchanting day; lots of loving couples, elderly ramblers and dog enthusiasts strolling or briskly marching - but no Nick.

Where was he? What could even happen to him? He was already dead for crying out loud.

What if he'd gone into the light? Fuck, he sure picked a fine time! But why wander around here for 200 years and seek eternal peace today? Didn't I mean anything to him?

That thought stopped me in my tracks. Was I falling in love with an amorous ancient Spectre?

This must be imminent horrible death talking.

Still, where was he?

There was someone who would know.

I tripped down the rocky path to the water and arrived to find a pair of Mallards paddling in the shallows, and seaweed rotting in the summer sun.

William Lemoine was gone.

What the fuck? I now felt very alone. And despite the warm day, cold. I am not prone to anxiety, though today I had a better excuse than most.

Worse than anxious; missing my mom and dad, I felt abandoned. I should have known those two fucking apparitions would let me down.

Shivering under the sunlight, I climbed back to the wooded path and made my way back to the car. I'd visit Fredriches' house and spend my last few hours with Brittany.

2000 hours,
A creek mouth near Kingston

O it's Tommy this, and Tommy that,
and Tommy ow's your soul
But it's thin red line of heroes when
the drums begin to roll
Rudyard Kipling

Sergeant Tran wasn't happy; he would have preferred to stage an accident early in the day but like everyone else he carried on.

OPP cruisers, lights flashing, blocked the parkway, outside of Amherstview. They even turned over an empty truck and set it on fire. This setup allowed them to bring Fire and Rescue, and paramedics on site.

Quite a party was planned and everyone had a job.

Kerr parked his launch two klics south and east of the site, and Marie hovered back of him in a Search and Rescue helicopter. Truman monitored the site from monitors in a hastily rigged "war room" at Queens. Fredriche joined him at another computer terminal.

Doctor Diane Skanky Von Fuckface, and Smith the American observed from an improvised camouflage shelter that resembled a duck blind.

Special Forces dudes were hiding - somewhere - to make sure I found the shore after the eels were whacked.

What would kill the eels? Damned if I knew.

Brittany had gone silent when I walked in the door on Ellerbeck.

"Not dead yet," I said in a tone that didn't even convince me.

"Oh my God, Courtney." She was white. Her eyes stared into the middle distance and her neck swayed, as if loose on its hinges.

"This isn't helping, Brittany," I said. "You could make something up and say: 'You're going to be fine, Courtney'."

But curiosity got the better of me: "So? What do you see?"

"It's all a jumble. It doesn't make sense. I see death and fire; noise and fear."

"What kind of death – fish or people?"

"I can't tell... do you have to go? Can't they send a commando or something?"

"My doctoral thesis was about luring horny lampreys to their demise. I spent most of yesterday with the chemists and engineers putting this together."

She let it go. Her bright blue eyes came into focus and she re-engaged. She pointed to a table.

"I need to feed you. If you're jumping in the water tonight, you'll need protein. I have locally raised free range goat with fresh leeks in a stew."

So here I was. Surrounded by help but in the end, alone. The canister of modified 3kPZS had been placed, and Diane provided me with the remote control unit. The air became strangely still.

"Good luck, Courtney," she said. "And hold onto the remote; we want it back."

I wanted to tell her to go fuck herself but just said: "Fine."

As I waded into the water everyone remaining onshore disappeared into hiding. The water had warmed during the day but remained chilly; oily and thick as it enveloped my thighs, moving towards my groin and body's core.

I attached the black box to a utility belt loosely worn over my swimsuit and swam out to the shoal. There, standing waist deep, I looked out into the deepening darkness, removed the remote and flicked the switch.

We had designed the canister to explode and disperse the pheromones. And while it was a big lake, even ordinary eels could pick up a few molecules miles away. These super eels would come from everywhere.

Though the night remained muggy, I realized I would need to stay loose, so I didn't freeze up when it was time to make my escape. I began to slowly flex my muscles until...

Imagine the lapping of a small brook over stones. Now turn up the volume.

Something moved; sinuously, stealthily, maybe two hundred metres out through the gloaming.

Here we go.

Fifteen thousand feet over Lake Ontario

Hell is empty, and all the devils are here.
Shakespeare

"Whatever happened to Weymann?"

Brigadier General Joe "Speedy" Gonzales, at the controls of the B2 bomber *The Spirit of Buffalo*, looked over to his co-pilot and mission commander, Colonel Veronica Mills.

"He's stocking shelves for a liquor store in Pensacola," she said. "You hit him pretty hard."

"Fuck him," Gonzales said, "The dumb son of a bitch tried to jump out of the plane over Syracuse. I should have stayed in my seat and waved goodbye. Give me a sitrep, Mills."

"We are to anticipate, locate, target and kill somewhere between 12 and 18 thirty metre hostile lamprey eels. They are being lured to the marked coordinates where they will cluster. Their positions will lock into the targeting computer, whereupon we will engage the plasma weapon to splash them."

"Assets on the surface?"

"The Canadians have covert soldiers on the ground, a coast guard vessel two klics out, and a helo in the air. We have a sub parked a three miles out, and one asset is in the water running the release canister."

"Combat Controller? Good, that helps."

"No sir, a scientist from some place called Scarborough."

"He'd better not cut and run on us."

"She."

Gonzales, with great effort, kept his groan to himself. He was old school but respected Colonel Mills too much to share his opinion on non-military women.

Mills added one more thing: "We should be grateful we're not in a Cessna this time."

She didn't see the smile under his helmet but Gonzales still needed to share his thoughts.

"I'm glad we get to clean up the mess, but we're still going fishing with one of the most sophisticated stealth bombers on the planet. We going to get all the slimy fuckers?"

"They only need to maintain a loose formation for a few seconds and the computer will have them locked. The new beam can thread a needle and melt a concrete bunker.

"We need the altitude and the stealth, these creatures have their own stealth technology and preternatural sensing."

"I'll line us up Mills, you kill them. Don't hesitate; we don't want to roast the girl."

"Yes sir."

Courtney

Petrified with fear, I couldn't count them as they rose from the water, undulating at great speed towards the canister. They were one horny pack of killer eels and they were going to be sooo pissed when no one was there for them to fuck.

They told me to stay until after they were killed. Any movement or sound might distract them. So I remained rooted on the sandbar, the remote box in my hand.

The Spirit of Buffalo

"Eighteen hostiles located sir… computer acquiring…we have a firing solution…locked…"

Courtney

I couldn't see a damn thing except this rolling black serpentine mountain of eel. So fucking big.

The remote vibrated, then emitted a shrill high pitched shriek.

What the fuck!

The Spirit of Buffalo

"Fire! Beams to targets; shit sir, one of the eels is turning away; we've lost our lock on it!"

Courtney

I don't know what was up there but scarlet arrows rained from heaven. I fell back in the lake, then stood again. Please God save me from this. The creatures reared madly and writhed when struck. A few burst into flames. The water grew warm and stunk with the wake of multi-tons of cooked and shredded fish.

Spirit of Buffalo

"Sir, we splashed all but one…. Goddam it to hell; I can't lock on it; it's too close to the asset. I don't know what to do!"

"I do." Gonzales grinned under his helmet.

Oh shit, now what have I done? Mills thought.

Gonzales executed a hard bank to port and began his dive.

Courtney

The last eel slowed as it approached, as if in reproach, honing in on the sound. I almost apologised, but what would I say? "Sorry all your friends thought they'd get laid and were parboiled instead."

That wouldn't stop it from consoling itself with a snack.

I considered tossing away the control which continued to shriek like a banshee on meth. But it wouldn't go far and the noise would be worse underwater.

As the head emerged from the lake my blood ran cold. I thought that was only an expression and, whoa - fuck - hair began to rise on my head.

The remote vibrated again and in a shower of sparks shorted out. Both the lamprey and I stood in silence and confusion, but for only a moment.

Someone was screaming on shore.

The eels' head turned; we both saw what was making the noise.

Diane Naylor and Smith stood speechless and confused as the creature stared. Beside them - screaming like the fucked up ghouls they were - stood the legion of the dead.

Nick was shouting and so was Phil. Even old Lemoine waved his bottle and cried like he was charging into battle.

The slime monster from hell turned away from me and began to wriggle towards the cacophony. Then it picked up speed.

Diane and Smith froze in horror.

The Sprit of Buffalo

If Veronica Mills had been amazed with what Gonzales could do with a Cessna Caravan; it had nothing on him diving a B2 bomber at 600 miles per hour. They were pulling so many Gs' she thought she'd swallow her teeth.

An urgent voice sounded through the static from mission control.

"Brigadier, we're getting orders to stand down, let the last one go."

"Fuck that, our asset's at risk." At least she tried. He was nothing if not loyal to the troops. But he wasn't finished.

"Weapons to manual," he screamed into the mic.

"What!" she said, "you'll never…" but she shut up, and did it. There was no talking to him now. The water approached so fast they might have been in free fall.

Gonzales hit the switch.

"Smile, you son of a bitch!"

Veronica laughed.

Courtney

More arrows from the sky… the eel in flames… I had to get to shore… shaking…something black like a monstrous bat eclipsed the moon and the stars, then disappeared again with a thunderous roar. I had to swim…

Tired … no strength, the water deepened. I didn't know if I would make it, men diving from shore… going under… sinking…

Noise above, rotors … no peace…a heavy splash… more lampreys…going down… strong arms embracing, and a thick grunt.

"Hey girlfriend, come to mama; this is the last time I pull your ass out of the drink."

2200 hours

Onshore

It is good for a man to invite his ghosts into his warm interior, out of the wild night, into the firelight, out of the howling dark.
A.S. Byatt

Forever had passed since I had entered the water. I lay on a gurney, wrapped in a blanket, exhausted but not too exhausted to argue with the paramedic.

"I'm not going to the hospital – not happening. Nothing's injured or broken, so piss off." He sighed and stepped away. All he could do is try.

Truman called Marie back to the war room for a debriefing, leaving me in the hands of the med techs.

Tran and Kerr - who had landed, told me the story. An American bomber with some kind of sci-fi weapon had killed the eels. One had almost escaped, but the pilot put his plane into a dive and hit it on the run.

They'd flown away to a secret hangar, with their secret plane, with its secret weapon.

Thanks, whoever you were.

Marie had ordered the Navy to move in and hover over me; without ceremony she jumped and kept me afloat until the Special Forces guys reached me.

I'd been raving but a quick exam by the paramedics showed nothing major was amiss.

Now, I carefully sat up and tried to stand.

It took a moment, but the dizziness passed and the fog cleared. Everything around me seemed unnaturally quiet.

"I'm going to take a walk to the water," I said. "Don't worry if I'm talking to myself."

Captain Lemoine greeted me with his usual formality: "Miss Courtney; it gives me great pleasure to find you well and about. You must forgive me, but having discharged my duty, I must return to my post on the lake."

I curtsied, and following a deep pull from his bottle for the road (or ether) and a tip of his toque, he disappeared.

Saying goodbye to Phil was more difficult. I could tell from the way he stood that he saw the light.

"Thanks," I said, "I appreciate your sticking around. I'd hug you if I it was possible."

He smiled sadly. "I wish you the best, Courtney; my husband's waiting for me on the other side. He died of cancer last year. That's why I came back to Kingston. Now we can be together."

And he was gone.

Husband? Yikes, did I call that wrong!

When I turned to hide my tears, Nick was waiting.

"I like Phil; cool dude. I told him and Lemoine if we worked together, we could short out that noise making contraption in your hands. Sorry it took so long. That old fathead Lemoine took forever to get it right, but Phil nailed it in one.

"You did that?"

"We did it together. Give old Lemoine credit where credit is due; when the clarion call to action sounded, he answered.

"Something had to be done; Naylor and that brigand Rogers planned for you to be killed by the eel. She had a young fuck buddy who was going to get your job."

"Rogers?"

"Great great grandson of that murderous rogue who killed me. Called himself Smith here."

I wanted so much to hug him.

And sorry I doubted his loyalty and friendship. Looking out at the blackness over the lake, I forced myself, through tears, to say the words on my mind:

"What about you Nick? Are you going into the light? Don't you miss Charlotte?"

For a moment that look of unbearable sadness I'd seen the first day flashed into his eyes; then - to my shock - he broke into a falsetto:

"Nicholas, I need a new frock!"

"Nicholas, feed the ducks!"

"Nicholas, fetch my mother in the pony cart."

"Not tonight Nicholas, I feel an ague coming on."

I laughed despite myself.

"I loved Charlotte but she made a week on the farm feel like eternity. I can't imagine what real eternity would be like. If I dare show my face in the hereafter, she'll be waiting with a honey-do list.

"I'm going back to the park for a spell; always lots of juicy gossip in the summer."

An awkward pause followed. He looked away shyly, then spoke again.

"You'll come by and visit me?"

I wanted that as much as he did.

"Yes Nicholas. It will be my pleasure."

"Ma'am you okay?" I turned; one of the army medics stood looking at me carefully. "I'm here to take you home."

"I'll be right there." He stepped back.

"Don't say anything," Nick said, "I don't want you taken to the bughouse like poor Maracle, but look down to the point.

"The last lamprey to go fell right on top of us. Phil, Lemoine and me; no worries, but those two - how would you like to spend eternity with them?"

Doctor Diane and Smith aka Rogers were going at it hammer and tongs.

"This is your fault Rogers; it's the girl who's supposed to be dead not me!"

"I'm dead too you dumb cow."

"You should be - it's your goddam fault!"

"My fault! You brought the broken remote."

"It worked when I tested it."

Nick and I shared another laugh. This probably sounded like encroaching hysteria to the medic, so I smiled at Nick and turned away to leave.

It had been a long week.

Monday, July 17

For before this I was born, once a boy, and a maiden,
and a plant, and a bird and a darting fish in the sea.
The Fragments

My phone rang early. I remained tired and everything still hurt. Taped boxes, empty bottles, and unwashed clothes lay about my apartment. Who the fuck was this? I had told Fredriche I was taking the week off and Brittany knew I was sleeping in.

"Good morning girlfriend!"

Oh good grief - who else but the mad commander.

"Marie, it's seven am."

Her voice changed. It lowered before she spoke again:

"An *Enteroctopus dofleini*, at least ten times the normal size, dragged a ferry full of Chinese tourists to the bottom of the ocean outside of Esquimalt last night.

"A military transport will land in six-zero minutes at Kingston airport. We need you."

"Ten times the normal size? That's a big fucking Octopus."

"Don't worry about packing, girlfriend. I have everything you need and can send a car to get you.

"You coming, Courtney? You know you want to."

Kingston airport had been built beside Lemoine Point.

I needed to make a stop, and say goodbye to a special friend who couldn't be reached later by phone.

"I'll meet you there in ninety minutes."

I didn't have to think. I'd miss Nick but she was right. My life had changed forever.

The end

Postscript

Tuesday, July 18

Pacific Ocean, somewhere near Esquimalt

0700 hours

"I need to find out the time when the octopus was first spotted. What's she saying?"

"Dammit, I don't know; did you ask a yes or no question?"

I was standing on the deck of a RCN launch talking to a fiftyish Chinese woman and Lieutenant Lucas Cheng.

Lieutenant commander, Marie Lesage sat observing to one side.

I was the only one having difficulty standing in the rocking launch. This wasn't Lake Ontario.

Cheng spoke to the woman in Cantonese; both had origins in Hong Kong. She wanted to help.

He asked his question again but differently. This time she nodded.

"She nodded. What did you ask her?"

"I asked if it struck after eight o'clock."

Now he asked a longer question. She supplied a longer answer, arms extended to both sides.

"What's she saying?" Cheng asked.

"I have no idea; she has her arms extended." Cheng was almost hopping with frustration.

"Sound out her words."

"Are you serious?"

"It's the only way." I repeated what I had heard. The woman put her hands over her ears and made a face. Cheng looked appalled.

"My God, and they say we have accents. Is that the best you can do?"

I was about to respond, but the woman looked into the sky and spoke. I turned back to Cheng.

"She's saying something that sounds like "wum" or "tung"."

"She might be saying something about light,"

By the time I swiveled back she had departed.

"Fuck, she's gone into the light," I said. "We've lost her to eternal peace and serenity."

Cheng threw his hands in the air. Marie started laughing.

"Girlfriend, you two looked so fucking stupid talking to a ghost."

He couldn't come down on a superior officer but Cheng looked serious as we faced Marie.

"I need to know the tentacle length. We need that intel for our profile." Marie laughed again.

What was I doing in the middle of the Pacific Ocean with this crazy bitch?

"They're about twenty-five meters long," she said.

"How do you know that?"

"Turn around and see for yourself."

Oh shit, really - again?

"...and hold on to something."

She jumped to her feet and screamed: "Ensign Rivers! Gun it! Full throttle. That's an order, sailor."